PRAISE FOR **Belle Isle**

"Rod Lockwood has written an amazing book. *Belle Isle* champions freedom and opportunity, the powers that attracted so many adventurous souls to America over the years. In *Belle Isle*, he helps us rediscover the roots that built this great nation and suggests that these great powers might once again work their magic, this time for Detroit, for Michigan, and perhaps even once again for the country we love."

—**HAL SPERLICH,** FORMER PRESIDENT, CHRYSLER CORPORATION, AND MEMBER OF THE AUTOMOTIVE HALL OF FAME

"As a non-American, I have to say that Rod Lockwood's inspiring book has a relevance that reaches far beyond the borders of the USA. It has lessons for all of us living in any Western democracy, with its inevitable bureaucratic compromises and, often, its complacency. His fresh proposals as to how we might rise above the daily restrictions and penalties under which we all live, and which often limit both our ability to find success and our motivation to do so, should make *Belle Isle* required reading for politicians throughout the supposedly free world."

—**SIMON TAYLOR,** FORMER CHAIRMAN, HAYMARKET MAGAZINES, UK; FORMULA 1 RACE ANNOUNCER FOR RADIO AND TV ON BBC AND ITV; PLAYED HIMSELF IN THE RACE MOVIE *RUSH*

"When given the opportunity, free from overbearing government regulations and restrictions, individuals will outperform the decisions made by bureaucrats. Nowhere is that more evident than in Rod Lockwood's story of the transformation of *Belle Isle*. Central planners and obstructionists be damned—and stay far, far away. Bold actions are needed to transform Detroit, and Lockwood's vision lays the groundwork to make it all happen."

—**MANNY LOPEZ,** AWARD-WINNING JOURNALIST AND FORMER OPINION EDITOR, *DETROIT NEWS*

"Change requires us to think differently. Detroit has been changed by Cadillac, Woodward, and Henry Ford in the past. Rod Lockwood's vision and passion for Detroit and its citizens are the changes we need for the future. I hope the people who decide will see the vision for what it is—finally real freedom and opportunity for us Detroiters, the chance of a lifetime to let us share in the American Dream. And we need it now."

—**LARRY MONGO,** OWNER, CAFE D'MONGO'S SPEAKEASY IN DETROIT, AND ENTREPRENEUR

"Aristotle wrote that 'the soul never thinks without a picture.' Rod's book paints a vivid picture of the impact the *Belle Isle* concept would have on individual lives and standards of living—both on the island and in surrounding areas. Art, according to Aristotle, is supposed to consist of 'life as it could be or ought to be.' In this sense, Rod's book is most certainly art—the most effective medium for conveying concepts. As Detroit continues to decline in both population and capital, the likelihood of Rod's idea taking hold will most certainly increase."

—STEVE THOMAS, OWNER, VINTAGE DETROIT COLLECTION

"I found *Belle Isle: Detroit's Game Changer* to be cogent, interesting, well written, and easy to read. Much writing is focused and narrow; this book is broad in scope and outlines important ideas. As a university professor, I can see *Belle Isle* being used as a special resource in a class in macroeconomics, public administration, or strategy. I would ask the students to take one of the issues (education, health care, role of government) and contrast the issue as developed in the book with current practices. *Belle Isle* is about ideas and would prove to be a great learning tool."

—DR. NEIL BUCKLEW, FORMER PRESIDENT,
WEST VIRGINIA UNIVERSITY

"Rod Lockwood's *Belle Isle* laboratory creates a culture of beauty, optimism, and economic freedom that reawakens a once-powerful Detroit economy. Our beautiful island is the catalyst for his experiment—a chemistry that combines government and financial institutions that embrace individual opportunity, celebrate the growth of wealth, and unleash the extraordinary power of the human spirit."

—BILL VOLZ, FORMER DEAN, MIKE ILITCH SCHOOL OF BUSINESS,
WAYNE STATE UNIVERSITY

"Progress depends on freedom, courage, and imagination. Lockwood's *Belle Isle* is not another fig leaf to dress up the status quo. It is the sort of bold, outside-the-box thinking that promises to revitalize a region and inspire the whole country."

—LAWRENCE W. REED, PRESIDENT EMERITUS, FOUNDATION FOR
ECONOMIC EDUCATION

ROD LOCKWOOD

Belle Isle

DETROIT'S GAME CHANGER

SUBPLOT
an imprint of Amplify Publishing Group

SUBPLOT™
an imprint of Amplify Publishing Group

www.mascotbooks.com

Belle Isle: Detroit's Game Changer

About the covers
The front cover depicts a morning view of Belle Isle following its transformation from an uninhabited island in the Detroit River to a magnet for capital, a dynamic new community founded on the principles of freedom and opportunity. The back cover shows a typical evening street scene in the downtown area of Belle Isle, a vibrant walking community. The covers show what can happen in Belle Isle and, in the process, transform Detroit into a dynamic city of its own, replacing destitution and dole with dignity and jobs. Let freedom ring.

Illustrations by L. Ryder

For more information, please contact:
Subplot Publishing, an imprint of Amplify Publishing Group
620 Herndon Parkway, Suite 220
Herndon, VA 20170
info@amplifypublishing.com

Library of Congress Control Number: 2025905073
CPSIA Code: PRV0525A
ISBN-13: 979-8-89138-473-6

Printed in the United States

My close friend Harold "Hal" Sperlich recently passed away on January 20, 2025, at the age of 95.

In memory of Hal, I dedicate this book to him.

His inspiration has moved me from simply writing an entertaining tale to making an all-out effort to bring Belle Isle *home. As he wrote in the foreword, Hal truly believed that Belle Isle would be the difference-maker for Detroit and beyond.*

Hal was a former president of Chrysler and the father of the Mustang, the minivan, and the K-car, among others, and was inducted into the Automotive Hall of Fame in 2009 with the accolade "Greatest Automotive Product Designer of the 20th Century." He was a genius.

So when Hal Sperlich told me, "Do it, and it can be done!", I have to believe him.

CONTENTS

FOREWORD

By Hal Sperlich

Former president, Chrysler Corporation,
and member of the Automotive Hall of Fame

When I was given the opportunity to read *Belle Isle*, I couldn't put it down. It was two hours of reading with amazement that someone could visualize a solution to one of America's most significant urban problems, poverty, along with its associated issues of drug abuse, homelessness, and crime. This plan would finally give many of the long-suffering people of Detroit a big shot at the American Dream. The solution would be based on the same principles on which our nation was founded: freedom, opportunity, and the self-reliance of the people.

The dynamism and success of any society reflect its basic principles. In Belle Isle's case, individual freedom and self-reliance, along with a small government that exists primarily to facilitate these values, provide the context within which men and women can reach the upper limits of their potential. As such, Belle Isle and the city of Detroit would be a magnet for capital and would become one of the most attractive places to work or do business in the world. With billions of private investment, without a penny of taxpayer money, this endeavor would launch a construction boom of enormous size and duration. This area would become a shining example of how capitalism can work, creating a beautiful, safe city with more jobs for its residents.

Belle Isle could become the economic miracle Rod Lockwood has envisioned if all the interested parties could agree. Would the city of Detroit, the state of Michigan, and the federal government go for this? The expected first reaction is probably not. Too big an idea. Undoubtedly, there will be the usual cries that Belle Isle would provide just one more advantage for the wealthy. But as Americans begin to realize how the development of Belle Isle could transform the lives of so many, they will come to understand that the power of freedom benefits all.

Finally, might this great social and economic experiment provide inspiration to our nation, which has strayed so far from the path of freedom and self-reliance laid out for us by our Founding Fathers?

It's an enormously interesting possibility.

INTRODUCTION

The United States of America is in trouble. Americans have lost faith in their elected officials. Label someone as a "politician" with time in "Washington," and their poll numbers plummet. The right and left have moved further from the center, causing deep divisions. Incessant personal attacks have replaced frank and honest discussion of policies. The majority of our citizens, the "middle class," have not fared well economically in the last decade. Retirees see their pensions in jeopardy as lifespans increase. Workers have lost an increasing portion of their paycheck, while those receiving government payouts are in a cycle of dependency with no way out, losing their dignity in the process.

Detroit is the leading indicator of the problems of the country.

In 1950 Detroit was a vibrant city, the wealthiest in the nation. Today the city has lost most of its population and wealth. Many good people have worked hard to improve Detroit, and their progress should be recognized. The Downtown, Midtown, and Corktown areas of Detroit have seen resurgence, but Detroit continues to suffer from an eroding tax base, causing high tax rates without a strong solution on the horizon. It may have passed the point of offering real hope for its struggling people. A new idea is needed, a dramatic act that has the power to turn all this around. This book is about that dramatic act, Detroit's game changer, which can become America's game changer as well.

The setting is Belle Isle, twenty-nine years in the future. It is fiction, but the main characters are real people whose names have been changed to protect their identities. Darin is one of the most creative people I know. He has the rare combination of a keen sense of aesthetics and a fiery passion for individual liberty and freedom. I can see him pulling this off. His dear friend Joe will make his mark in the world, too, but in this book, it is in another country.

Belle Isle is an island in the Detroit River owned by the city of Detroit. It is uninhabited and recently became a state park, under lease to Michigan. It may be the most important 982 acres in the state of Michigan, perhaps in the entire country. What Darin does with Belle Isle is remarkable in itself, but even more important, Belle Isle can turn around Detroit and beyond. Belle Isle's culture of unlimited opportunity, fueled by a culture of "can do" optimism, will create a firestorm of jobs and wealth creation. The sparks will jump the river and start similar fires in Detroit and Southeast Michigan. The light from those fires may even show the way for our country to once again find the power of freedom on which it was founded.

This book is not about creating an island of wealth, even though it does. Of course it will attract wealth, and wealth is fine, but what will distinguish it from other city-states or special economic zones are its spirit and optimism. Even the less wealthy will bask in the sunshine of freedom and be lifted by its opportunity. Unfettered from too many rules and regulations, from taxing the wrong things, from inefficient, self-serving government, Belle Isle will become the "Midwest Tiger," rivaling Singapore, Shenzhen, and Hong Kong in its economic miracle.

As a lover of liberty and a believer in the human fabric, I have, over the years, observed a slow crawl toward the lowest common denominator. Not that society here in the United States used to be perfect, but there are many tangible examples of a deterioration of the quality of life, even as the standard measures of material wealth have greatly increased. Over the last sixty years, the inflation-adjusted gross domestic product per capita has increased more than threefold. That is good. The opportunities for women and minorities have greatly increased. That is good. But think of all the behaviors and norms that exist today, which in many cases did not sixty years ago. We fear for our safety, and many of us don't venture into many parts of Detroit. Concealed weapon permits are considered and often obtained. We blame others for our mistakes and poor judgment. If we slip and fall for most any reason, our first thought is not how careless we were but whether we should call an attorney. We buy lottery tickets with our hard-earned money to give us some hope, even though we know the "average return" is, at best, 50 percent. We don't trust or believe in our government, particularly Washington, to do the right thing. We believe Washington answers to special interests, which exact favors from elected officials in exchange for funding their reelection campaigns. Our country is badly divided. The left and right aren't talking, and when they speak, the language is full of ad hominem attacks. We have lost hope.

This book is about fixing that—about creating a social laboratory that takes new approaches in the areas of government services, taxation, labor, money, and legal systems, among others. To give credit, many of the ideas are not mine; they are ones that I have heard about over the years that have stuck with me as making sense. I hope the reader understands I am not seeking to claim them as my own. I simply subscribe to the notion that true power arises from meaning—meaning that uplifts and enables. Witness the fact that Mahatma Gandhi brought down British colonialism without raising his hand in anger. Rather, it was the power of selflessness, faith in the intrinsic dignity of man, and our divinely acquired rights to freedom, sovereignty, and self-determination. And so this shall be the power that gives rise to the miracle of Belle Isle.

So, dear reader, I hope you enjoy your journey into the future and join me in imagining how the shining light of Belle Isle can save Detroit and show the way for the United States as well.

Chapter 1

JOE'S ARRIVAL

Excellence is the result of caring more than others think is wise, risking more than others think is safe, dreaming more than others think is practical, and expecting more than others think is possible.

—Ronnie Oldham

The late-afternoon sun made it difficult for Joe to recognize all the old landmarks.

Putting his sunglasses on helped, and the Renaissance Center came into view as the shuttle helicopter moved eastward north of the Detroit River toward its destination.

Man, how different Detroit looks, Joe thought.

Minicities surrounded by large areas of parks and urban gardens had replaced the sprawling neighborhoods he remembered from his youth. Joe had read about Detroit and how it had been transformed from a single large city of decay to a collection of smaller cities, each with its own identity. Even the names were different. He couldn't remember them all, only Indian Village, Eastside Village, Corktown, Woodbridge, and Palmer Woods. There were others; perhaps Darin would know.

It had been twenty-five years since Joe had been to Detroit. After graduating from Michigan State and getting an MBA from Wayne State, Joe started his career in the biotech industry.

Initially working in Boston for a start-up, he moved to the company's home base in Slovakia after its success. Joe rose in its rank to chief operating officer. With an international market, Joe was often traveling.

People liked Joe.

He was born and raised in Michigan by his Syrian parents. His given name was Yousef Sharif, but Yousef, being Arabic for Joseph, quickly became Joe. He was tall, over six feet two inches, with an athletic build, blond hair, and blue eyes. Women thought he was gorgeous, and men were immediately put at ease by his friendly nature.

Life had slowed down a bit from the years of eighty-hour workweeks. He had trained his staff well, and his number two guy (who was actually a woman) kept the company running just as well as, perhaps even better than, when Joe was there. Now at fifty-eight, he was able to take some time off.

Darin and Joe had kept in touch, although Joe hadn't seen his old high school buddy since he had gone off to Slovakia. They followed each other's careers with great interest.

Darin attended the University of Michigan and graduated with a degree in architecture and later earned a master's in urban design at the same institution. Darin was the most creative person Joe had ever met, excelling in art and music in his youth. Darin had an eye for shape and color and could quickly size up what looked good. Joe chuckled, remembering that in high school some of the girls would take Darin shopping with them as their fashion consultant when buying clothes.

After getting his master's, Darin worked for an international urban design firm affiliated with the Universiti Teknologi Malaysia. Their assignment was to plan the expansion of a part of the government-sponsored city-state of Malacca in Malaysia. Malacca had been granted independence from Malaysia and had international funding, primarily from Singapore, to reconstruct a model city.

As a junior project manager, Darin studied under Savas Sahin, the great Turkish planner. The two worked well together and melded the disciplines of urban planning and governance, achieving worldwide recognition as Malacca started its growth into the megalopolis it was today.

But Darin had his own siren song. At thirty, a group of investors contacted him and offered him a position to head up the planning and development of Belle Isle, an island in the Detroit River, purchased from the city of Detroit.

Every year Darin invited Joe to come back and visit. Joe read long emails from Darin, pleading for him to check out the transformation of Belle Isle from an island park to a thriving metropolis. Joe inevitably responded he was just too busy with his Slovakia duties; perhaps next year.

But a *TIME* magazine article pushed him over the edge, and now twenty-some years later, Joe came home to reunite with his friend and see for himself what Darin had accomplished.

The helicopter made a right turn to the south, and Belle Isle came into view. Once a largely abandoned city park, it was now teeming with buildings of all shapes and sizes, with brick-laid streets interspersed with parks and green spaces. The tallest building was the fifty-seven-story Four Seasons hotel, and the helicopter aimed for the hotel's helipad.

As the rotor blades wound down, Joe let the other shuttle passengers disembark first. They seemed in a hurry, and he was not. There were three young, well-dressed men in business suits, all carrying satchels, and an attractive middle-aged woman who appeared to be Middle Eastern. Tired from the long trip from Slovakia to New York and then on to Detroit, Joe was exhausted. Porters dressed in black suits with white shirts unloaded the helicopter in the afternoon breeze. One hefted Joe's black leather suitcase onto a cart emblazoned with the Four Seasons logo, which was Joe's signal it was time to step outside. A warm July breeze greeted him.

Darin hadn't changed much. Tall and thin but muscular with dark-brown hair, he stood waiting near the small roof pad terminal. He was dressed in a light blue Polo shirt and beige slacks, wearing classic Ray-Ban sunglasses. He looked like his picture in the *TIME* magazine article. Embedded in the piece was a shot of Darin standing on the Four Seasons roof, facing the camera, with Belle Isle in the background. The caption on the photo was "Nation Builder." Joe thought it was a bit much, but *TIME* always exaggerated everything—it was good for business.

They embraced and sized each other up. Almost three decades had added maturity to both but had not robbed them of their youthful good looks.

"Joe, man, you look great. Not changed a bit."

"Darin, you too. I think growing older agrees with you. Where's the gray hair?"

"None yet. Maybe someday. I'm still trying to eat healthy and do the right things to keep in shape. Also, we do a lot of walking here, which helps."

Inside the helipad terminal, Joe's suitcase and the porter who grabbed it had already disappeared. Darin saw Joe's concerned look and said, "Don't worry. I had them check you in before your arrival. You're in the von Mises Suite—fifty-fifth floor with an incredible view. Should be comfortable." He handed Joe his room key. "Should we grab a drink at the bar, or do you want to check out your room first? I'm sure you're exhausted."

"A drink sounds nice. Only if you're buying, though." Joe smiled. Their long separation hadn't robbed them of their natural ease with each other.

The Skyline Bar was on the fifty-sixth floor of the hotel, spanning the entire east end of the floor and commanding three views. To the north was Detroit, with the downtown off to the left and Jefferson directly across the river; to the south was Windsor, Canada; and to the east was most of Belle Isle, with its collection of parks and residences and the Detroit River stretching toward its mouth at Lake St. Clair. The scenes were stunning.

The hostess seated them at a sectional sofa facing the window with the east view of Belle Isle. The atmosphere in the Skyline Bar was minimalistic, yet what few pieces decorated the space felt opulent. The bar itself was a long, curved counter made of polished marble, illuminated from beneath to give it a futuristic feel. The seating was plush and comfortable, featuring sleek leather couches and chairs arranged in small clusters. The fabrics were a meld of greens and red wine, which complemented the Verde marble cocktail tables. The outside walls were composed almost entirely of glass, stretching to the top of the ten-foot ceiling. Cherry beams divided the ceiling into four-foot squares, finished with stucco and a faint beige wash. The glass walls were interrupted every eight feet by a wood column, in the same finish as the ceiling beams. A large fireplace, trimmed with a marble surround and hearth, dominated the west wall. Over the fireplace was a painting of a sailboat regatta. It appeared to Joe that each seating area was individually done. The look was both elegant and cozy.

The hostess summoned the waiter.

"Mr. Fraser, the usual, sir?"

"Come on, Michael. What's this Mr. Fraser stuff?" Darin turned to Joe. Pointing to the waiter, he said, "I've known Michael for at least ten years. He used to work at the Book Cadillac hotel in Detroit. I almost begged him to come work on Belle Isle about five years ago. He's served me more drinks than I can count, and now he pulls the formal thing on me. What, do you think I need to impress my friend here? Michael, meet Joe Sharif. He has come all the way from Slovakia to see us."

"Very nice to meet you." He asked again, "The usual?"

"No, it's a little early for that. I'll take an iced tea with lemon."

"Of course. Mr. Sharif, you have come quite a long way, sir. May I interest you in a glass of wine or something stronger perhaps?"

Joe, being Muslim, didn't drink and ordered iced tea too.

The teas arrived with some raspberry scones, not ordered but much appreciated. Over the drinks the two friends caught up on the essentials of family, friends, and work. Darin outlined the agenda for Joe.

"I have dinner reservations for us tonight at seven. That gives you a couple of hours to rest and clean up. Meet me in the lobby of the hotel about six thirty, and we'll go from there. I have scheduled the days ahead starting at midmorning. That leaves your early mornings free to communicate with Slovakia before they close down. Your suite has full communications, including video feed, so you shouldn't miss too many beats. Today we relax, and tomorrow we'll start the tour. I can't tell you how excited I am to show you everything we've done here. I think you'll find it very, very interesting."

"Darin, I really appreciate you taking the time to show me around.

You must have better things to do than be my host."

"You bet I do. I'm soooo busy!" Darin chuckled. "No, seriously, when my best friend, whom I haven't seen in years, comes back to see me, it's a big deal. We have a lot of catching up to do. This is my life's work. There's nothing I want to do more than show it off. There is an energy level here that I have never seen in any other part of the world. You might call it a 'can do' attitude. You will meet many fine people. And the residents of Belle Isle are anxious to meet you. Our *Belle Isle Blog*, one of our most popular news sources, has run a few pieces on your visit for the past week, so don't be surprised if you are recognized on the street."

Chapter 2

THE FOUR SEASONS

Freedom is never more than one generation away from extinction . . . It must be fought for, protected, and handed on for them to do the same, or one day we will spend our sunset years telling our children and our children's children what it was once like in the United States when men were free.

—Ronald Reagan

The von Mises Suite was one floor below the Skyline Bar. Entering through a marble foyer, the room opened up into the living room with a fireplace and a large TV alcove. An emerald-green couch and leather chairs surrounded a glass-topped coffee table with a brushed metal base. In the corner was a large intricately carved mahogany desk paired with a high-back leather chair, deep burgundy in color. Behind the chair was an oil portrait of a distinguished-looking man with thin white hair and a mustache. "Could this be von Mises?" Joe mused. Adjacent was a full kitchen with a bar. Past the living room was an office with state-of-the-art electronics, including a 3D videoconference screen. Two queen-size beds, chairs, and ottomans filled the bedroom. Off the bedroom and wrapping around to the living room was a balcony with seating for four around a bronze-and-glass table. Joe estimated one could entertain about twelve to fifteen people comfortably. He wondered who von Mises was; he would be sure to ask Darin.

The suite had two views. To the east was Belle Isle, and beyond the Detroit River was Lake St. Clair. A sailboat regatta was underway on the lake, and most of the boats had their colorful spinnakers up. A few powerboats were motoring by, and on the distant horizon, Joe could see a giant iron-ore carrier making its way westbound in the ship channel.

To the north Joe saw a monorail spanning across the river that disappeared into a five-story parking deck. A large park lay to the east of the monorail on the Detroit side of the river, highlighted by a tall Ferris wheel. To the northeast Joe could see on the horizon an airport with a single long runway, surrounded by factories, warehouses, hangars, and a large terminal building. Airplanes of all sizes dotted the tarmac. Joe had once been to the Detroit City Airport in his youth, but it had been run-down. Could this be the same airport?

Joe's two-hour slumber was interrupted by the hotel's front desk call to remind him of his dinner appointment. He quickly showered, dressed in black slacks and a white linen short-sleeved shirt, and slipped on casual leather walking shoes. Darin had said to keep it comfortable.

He was seated at the lobby bar, holding a seat open for Joe. Waters were already sitting on the bar top, which was a large continuous aquarium. Under the drinks, small bass and walleye swam lazily by. Darin commented with a smile that they were all local fish, no exotic imports.

The bar of the lobby was full with men and women of all ages engaged in deep conversation. An outdoor seating area off the bar overlooked the Detroit River and Canada. A large yacht with a Bahamian flag motored lazily upstream, its aft deck filled with couples gawking at the island, with the hotel's patio guests returning polite stares.

The lobby of the Belle Isle Four Seasons was both modern and timeless. The ceilings soared far above him, supported by grandiose marble columns, each one crowned with intricately carved capitals that shimmered in the soft, ambient lighting. The floor was also marble, matching the columns. Joe had extensively traveled in his work and stayed at some of the best hotels in Europe. To him, the Four Seasons lobby had the feeling of old-world grandeur but adapted to today's world with its tall ceiling and a monorail station overhead. Suspended from the ceiling was a series of small Fresnel lenses, their intensity subdued, but the horizontal lights produced a dazzling display on the high wall of the lobby. Joe recognized the lenses as similar to the one he had seen in the Cana Island lighthouse in Door County, Wisconsin. He wondered if there was symbolism in its choice. Possibly lighting the way to prosperity? If first impressions meant anything, Joe was sold. A group that could build this could do anything. He started to wonder if he might want to be a part of it.

A whooshing sound overhead brought Joe's attention to the monorail, which was a good twenty-five feet above the lobby floor and just gliding to a stop. An escalator ran from the lobby floor up to the monorail's loading platform.

Darin noticed Joe's gaze. "Don't worry. Another will be by in a couple of minutes. We'll catch the next one."

Chapter 3

MONORAIL

The American Republic will endure until the day Congress discovers that it can bribe the public with the public's money.

—Alexis de Tocqueville

As they waited for the next monorail, Darin explained the transportation system.

"We have two rails. One runs only on the island and is called Island Shuttle, and the other, the Transportation Shuttle, goes to the Transportation Center, which is off-island on the Detroit side of the river. The Island Shuttle runs counterclockwise within the island and has eleven stops. There are five cars running the route. To do an entire loop with the stops takes about thirteen minutes, so the average transit time is about half that. The stops include the Residential districts, of which there are three, and the Restaurant/Entertainment areas—two there. We also have stops at the Financial District, the Market District, the Shopping District, the Sports Complex, the School/Worship District, and the Detroit Yacht Club.

"What we call the Transportation Shuttle has five stops on the island and then runs to the Transportation Center on the Detroit side of the river. That loop takes fourteen minutes to do a round trip, but the longest ride would be no more than ten minutes to get to the Transportation Center. It omits one of the Restaurant/Entertainment districts, the Market, Shopping, Sports, and School/Worship districts. Now if you want to get from one of those to the Transportation Center, you take the Island Shuttle to the next Transportation-served terminal and switch shuttles."

Their monorail appeared, and the two stepped through the doors. The car was half filled with people, most either talking among themselves or engrossed in smartphones.

Darin and Joe didn't bother to take a seat for the minute-or-so ride to the next stop. Besides, by standing, they could take in the view of the river on one side and the busy street filled with dinner-hour walkers on the other.

Joe commented, "When I was last here on Belle Isle many years ago, I could only walk around the area. It was pretty then, but now with this high-up view, it is simply breathtaking."

Darin replied, "Yes, that is one of the reasons we went with an elevated monorail rather than a subway. Everything we do here has an aesthetic consideration, and of course views are paramount. We spent hours upon hours doing computer mock-ups of what the monorail rider would see on the ride. Both the route and the building design were based on making it both interesting and beautiful. If you think about it, the monorail offers the highest amount of aesthetics in the shortest time, more than any other experience on the island. Walking views are important, too, of course. But when residents bring guests here, they often take the monorail around multiple times as sort of a tour! The other consideration was cost feasibility. A subway system would have been more expensive, and the soil conditions and dewatering issues would have been costly."

Chapter 4

LES DELICES

The smallest minority on earth is the individual. Those who deny individual rights cannot claim to be defenders of minorities.

—Ayn Rand

Back on the street, Darin and Joe made their way a block east to the Les Delices restaurant. Joe noted that the sidewalk was changing frequently in its use of materials. At times it was brick, then transitioned to slate, and then back to a different brick. In front of Les Delices, it was stone with brick accents. Joe found the variety interesting and charming.

Les Delices had a facade of stone, stucco, and brick. Diners were seated outside by the sidewalk, and Joe noted a second-floor patio with an outdoor bar. The hostess was dressed in a black cocktail dress and appeared to be of Asian descent. She knew Darin by name and led them to a private booth in the back.

Drinks were served, and Darin started his story.

"Joe, you remember my brother, Andrew. Well, he owns this restaurant and will be by to say hi at some point. I told him you were coming, and he wants to see you. Andrew always had an interest in cooking and food. You remember that little garden he used to keep?

Well, that passion exploded over the years, and he even invented a new strain of tomato. It's become quite popular. You should try one of the salads or tomato dishes tonight—they are quite unique. He also started a line of salsa that is manufactured in Detroit from tomatoes grown on an urban farm there and sold in five states. It's called Belle Isle Salsa and is very good. It's on the menu here, of course—I'll order it for us."

"So Andrew does all the cooking? Is this his full-time thing?"

"No, he has a chef, formerly from Brooklyn, but oversees the menu and occasionally dabbles in the kitchen. Most of his focus is spent on the family real estate operation that he took over from our father. It originally was only in Michigan but now has properties in the Midwest and Southeast US. The headquarters are right here on Belle Isle.

"I mentioned the chef is from Brooklyn. Belle Isle and Detroit have been a magnet for the artisan types previously sited in Brooklyn. The growth in Belle Isle and the relatively inexpensive land prices in Detroit have been real attractions.

"Also, one of the great things about this location, both for Andrew and for other businesspeople who live here, is the access to markets. Michigan used to be considered one of the 'fly-over' states—companies would headquarter on the coasts and do business on the other coast, fly over us, and we were largely ignored. That has changed. We now like to call ourselves the 'fly-from' state because by being in the middle, our travel time to all the markets is shorter. It makes our location more valuable, not less.

"For example, the family company has an apartment community located near Charleston, South Carolina, about ten minutes from the Charleston airport. The total travel time from the company office to the Charleston location is two and a half hours. That includes the monorail ride to the Detroit City Airport, the plane to Charleston, and the car ride on the other side. Of course that's on the company airplane. By contrast, if you were in Manhattan, the total time to Charleston would be about five hours on a commercial plane out of LaGuardia or four hours by corporate jet. From Los Angeles, add three hours to those numbers. Time is money."

"Hmm. I can see how being right in the middle of what is one of the world's largest economies is a big advantage. And despite the ubiquitous virtual world, we business folks know the value of face-to-face meetings and the need to travel. I can see it."

Joe toyed with the idea of an office here compared with the one they had in Boston. It certainly would cut down on travel time to the West Coast, Texas, and other markets they were trying to penetrate.

"But tell me about your work here."

Darin smiled. "Where do I start?"

"How about the beginning?"

Chapter 5

BELLE ISLE HISTORY

Much of the social history of the Western world over the past three decades has involved replacing what worked with what sounded good.

—Thomas Sowell

"Joe, you said you read the *TIME* article, so I won't spend time on every detail," Darin began. "But about twenty-eight years ago, a group of people my father knew, a loosely knit collection of free-market and liberty folks who called themselves the Friends of Liberty, came up with the idea of forming their own society. I suppose it would be easy to do so by buying some island in the Caribbean and negotiating independence, but that would be remote, both from a business standpoint and from a cultural standpoint too. Well, back in 2000, a free-market think tank based in Michigan called the Mackinac Center published an article titled 'For Whom the Private "Belle" Tolls' that proposed selling Belle Isle to private developers who would build a community free from the city of Detroit's regulations and taxes. Sort of do its own thing. The price to buy Belle Isle in the article was $370 million. The idea remained dormant for a few years, but as Detroit's recovery stalled, the idea came back to the surface. So they offered a billion dollars for the island, a little over $1 million per acre, which in today's US dollars is equivalent to $2.5 billion. But the investor group, as part of the offer and to be financially feasible, required Belle Isle become its own political jurisdiction, with its own laws, taxation, residency, everything.

"Although the city could use the money and the offer was very lucrative, there was a lot of opposition.

"Some Detroit groups were aghast. 'How *dare* you take away our jewel?' they would say. There were a lot of protests. But the leaders in Detroit saw the possibilities, not only what the money would do for Detroit, which badly needed funds for neighborhood relocation, but also how the new community would be a magnet for investment in the area.

"Critics at the time predicted all the superrich would move here to avoid their large tax bills, but they were wrong. Those people already had so much money *after* taxes that they didn't see the need to move. What we have seen is Belle Isle attracts younger people who are early in their careers with rising incomes and who want to build capital to grow their businesses. We also agreed to bring people from other countries to Belle Isle who would be job creators for Detroiters and, by doing so, increase tax collections and mitigate the effect of lost taxes by Americans moving here."

Darin continued, "Some worried if Belle Isle were allowed to form its own free city, others would want to follow. For example, Texas had a secessionist group that was quite vocal. 'If Belle Isle could do that, why can't we?' But we pointed out that Texas was having huge job and population growth and was doing just fine under its statehood status, while Detroit was a poor city looking for a solution. Also, we weren't leaving, just remaking ourselves.

"But the biggest group was the doubters, most who thought the idea was great but impossible to achieve. 'It can't be done,' 'You guys are crazy wackos,' and so forth. But the more people talked about it, the more the vision became clear. A place where people had unlimited opportunity and freedom. Where government got out of the way and didn't dictate how they should lead their lives. Where people were united in their common vision of opportunity, responsibility, honesty, and respect for each other. It was very powerful, and it was inevitable something major was going to happen."

Darin added, "Detroit had gone bankrupt. Emerging from bankruptcy, it still had money needs. The city of Detroit folks, along with some local nonprofits, put together a great plan on how to spend the billion dollars. Primary was relocation and consolidation to target areas of Detroit. The fact that the Belle Isle investors were going to spend another $4 billion on infrastructure and more than $20 billion in private construction was going to create a ton of jobs for Detroiters. And half the capital was going to come from outside the US, along with fifteen thousand immigrants from abroad. A top economic consulting firm studied the issue and predicted that Belle Isle would become a magnet for capital from all over the world, as its 10 percent cost of government would make it übercompetitive compared with the typical 40 percent in many of the Western economies. It turned out to be true. So the Friends of Liberty became the *Friends of Detroit*."

"You mentioned the Friends of Liberty were free-market liberty types. So is Belle Isle a libertarian-based society?" Joe asked.

"Who can say?" Darin answered. "We really resist labels here. Back when this idea got started, the US was extremely divided. Well, you know that—you were still here at that point. There were conservatives who despised the liberals as being freeloaders and simply wanting to take that which they hadn't earned or deserved. The liberals hated the conservatives as being uncaring for the less fortunate and puppets of the fat-cat millionaires and crony capitalists. Then you had the libertarians and Tea Party types who just wanted to be left alone and freed from intrusive government. But my point is that it is impossible to accurately label the complex views of life and society with single words. And to try to do so only introduces false perceptions of the beliefs of people. So we don't use those terms here. Of course we have our viewpoints, but we drill down to the specifics of the issue and are always looking for solutions. If you had to label us, we might be called *solutionists*."

Darin continued, "But being a solutionist doesn't make someone a pragmatist who sacrifices principles. Our community is built on three principles. The first is that our system of government is a value provider and only performs those functions that cannot be served well by a free people in a free market. The government is also highly transparent and works hard to be free of influence and corruption.

"The second principle is our community must have exceptional aesthetics. I'm talking about our architecture and planning. Although we believe we spend our money wisely here, we don't take the cheapest way out. We believe the aesthetic environment is as important as the water and air quality.

"Third, we respect all our residents, no matter what their station in life or our society. And we promote self-reliance, as freedom goes hand in hand with personal responsibility. We share a common ground here in the first two principles. We teach in our schools—voluntarily, I might add—that value-oriented government and the beauty of our surroundings are important core values that bind us, just like our English language."

"Why is English so important? Many countries have multiple languages."

"True, but we believe in understanding. Understanding others' viewpoints, wishes, and desires requires a common language. We don't always agree, but we always understand."

Darin continued with his story. "Initially, Washington was opposed for the reasons I mentioned before, but mostly they didn't want some tax haven that would suck revenue from the federal government, which, of course, seemed to have an insatiable appetite for finding money from any source.

"So what the Friends of Liberty did was offer to limit residency to fifty thousand people, which the Feds seemed to tolerate, and frankly, that's all we can fit on the island. Right now we're at about thirty-five thousand. They also agreed to make an annual payment to the federal government that would cover the defense costs of Belle Isle, the assumption being our security here depends on the US military. That number is calculated based on the per capita defense budget times the number of residents we have. We are probably paying too much, as the US is still embarking on foreign ventures from time to time that don't have any tangible defensive component, but we don't argue about it—we just pay it. In terms of the US dollar back twenty-eight years ago, it worked out to about $3,000 per person."

They were interrupted by a waiter, dressed entirely in black, with a cursive Les Delices emblazoned on his suit lapel. "Pardon me, Mr. Fraser, would you like to order an appetizer?"

Darin looked up. "Oh hi, Zharko. Any specials today?"

"Yes—we have seared scallops with truffle foam, accompanied by cauliflower puree, mushrooms, and a hazelnut beurre noisette. Also a Wagyu beef tenderloin with a red wine reduction, served with *pommes* Anna, glazed baby carrots, and black garlic puree."

"Okay, give us a few minutes, but we'll take some calamari for an appetizer. Joe, does that sound good?"

Joe nodded his assent.

"Zharko, what mocktails might you have for my friend Joe here?"

"We have a cucumber mint cooler and a very interesting mango mule."

Joe chose the mango mule.

Darin ordered his usual—a Maker's Mark bourbon Manhattan, up.

Joe reflected on what Darin had shared regarding starting Belle Isle. It seemed inconceivable that a city-state like this could happen, yet he had now seen it with his own eyes. The politics on getting approved must have been a challenge for sure, but the even more intriguing part was their success in attracting people to come here and build lives. He wanted to hear how that happened. He wondered what the biggest appeal was. No doubt it was related to economic freedoms.

The conversation resumed.

"So, Darin, how do you pay that tax? Or for that matter, what is your tax system?"

Chapter 6

TAXATION

It is no contradiction—the most important single thing we can do to stimulate investment in today's economy is to raise consumption by major reduction of individual income tax rates.

—John F. Kennedy

Darin answered, "It's a broad question, and one the Friends of Liberty and their advisors spent a lot of time debating. Now understand, this was before I was recruited to work on the project, so I'm not familiar with all the ideas that were discussed, only those that survived.

"There were some broad principles that governed. First and possibly most important, taxes had to be transparent. So the European model of a value-added tax was quickly discarded because it was added at different levels of production and is basically a hidden consumption tax, embedded in the price of the product.

"Second, we never tax that which we like to encourage. We want to create and have wealth, so we never tax the creation of wealth. So taxation of income or investment is off the table, and we never consider it. We have no tax on income, either personal or corporate. We have no inheritance tax. Death is penalty enough—there shouldn't be a tax on top of it! Now some countries, especially those that can't keep their spending under control, say we are a tax haven because we don't tax income or wealth creation, and we say if that's your definition of a tax haven, we are proud to be one."

"So you're not a tax haven?" Joe asked, clearly doubtful.

The drinks were served. Joe sipped his mango mule and gave a thumbs-up to Zharko. "Very good. What's in it?"

"Mango puree, lime juice, ginger beer, and that's a slice of fresh mango." Joe would have to remember that combination for later.

Darin continued, "No, we're a spending haven! Effective and efficient. Transparent and trustworthy. The taxes follow the spending, and we never borrow to support our spending. Politicians around the world talk about cutting taxes. Rarely do they talk about cutting spending. We start the conversation about spending.

"We encourage user fees. So if our government provides a service that is used only by certain people or groups, we charge for it. 'You get what you pay for, and you pay for what you get.' That is, provided the costs of collection are fair and efficient. For example, let's say we provide a service that is rather low priced, say one Midas, but it costs us half a Midas to collect the tax for that service. We would consider that inefficient, a 50 percent collection cost. We also consider whether the service is widely used or not when we decide whether to separately place a user tax or tax from the general fund."

Joe interrupted, "Darin, what is a Midas? Does Belle Isle have its own currency?"

"Yes, it does. It's a long story, so I'll get to it later, but back on taxation.

"Before we talk about what we do tax, let's spend time on what the government of Belle Isle provides. I talked about spending. First of all, we try to provide as little as possible. I know that sounds silly, but it really is based on the principle that the private sector inherently provides better service and a better product than does the government. That's because profit is a motivator. We love profit. On the plus side is what people are willing to pay for a good or service, provided it is done without coercion or subsidy, and the negative side is the amount of resources consumed. The net between the two is the good or the profit. If a process doesn't have profit, we look at it with deep and profound skepticism!"

Joe nodded his agreement. "You're right on. One of the things I see in Slovakia, which is perhaps a holdover from the Soviet era, is many people view businesses as greedy and see profit and greed as the same. But I don't get it."

"Joe, envy is not confined to Slovakia. It's part of the human condition. But we also acknowledge that profit without competition is worse than not making a profit at all. So if, for whatever reason, a process will be only provided by one company in the private sector, then our government will step in and either regulate the process or take it over completely. The regulatory option is preferable to the government option, of course. An example is the public power utility. We have a private company here that has built a small nuclear reactor using nuclear submarine technology, but we don't have enough of a population base to support another reactor owned by a second company. So we regulate the rates for the power. The rates are computed by a formula based on risk-adjusted return on capital with incentives for reliability, efficiency, and expense reduction. Some of our smart financial types came up with it, and the private power company is fine with it, and everyone is happy. We have the most reliable and lowest cost power in the area as a result. It works out very well. However, if a competitor came into the marketplace and built a second power plant, we would sell ours off to the private sector."

Their conversation was interrupted by the arrival of the appetizers; Joe ordered the scallops and Darin the beef. Joe noted the waiter wrote the order using a pen on a small pad of paper. He hadn't seen that in quite a while.

Darin continued, "Take, for example, our monorail. There's only room for one on Belle Isle, and the monorail is considered like a road or sidewalk—a necessary part of our community. It is a public utility. We have a combination of base fees and user fees. We take the initial capital cost of the monorail and the debt service required for the capital, and that gets paid from the general fund. However, the operating expenses, payroll, electricity, maintenance, etcetera are paid by user fees. Each of us has an ID on our phone that is recognized every time we use the monorail, which then translates to a quarterly bill. It is minor and amounts to a few Midas a month. Everyone uses the monorail and doesn't think twice about the cost."

As Darin spoke, Joe watched the monorail woosh by. From where they were sitting, Joe could see a good portion of the rail winding its way along the island. The ease with which people hopped on and off reminded him of his days back in Boston. He didn't own a car for years because the public transport was so good. It appeared people here felt the same way.

"Some of our general tax revenue comes from transaction or consumption taxes. So we basically have a sales tax on goods and services. It amounts to about 9 percent and is collected by the seller/provider and remitted to us on a monthly basis. One of the things we like about this tax is the ease and efficiency of the collection process. We have certain exemptions, primarily on the services side, but only for efficiency of collection issues. If the time spent on the collection/remitting typically takes over 25 percent of the tax collected, we have a review process for exempting that activity. It makes no sense to spend a lot of time on tax collection. This is one of the lessons we learned from the US government's ill-advised activities on the federal income tax. Its costs of collection and the taxpayer compliance and reporting costs were huge. I remember hearing back in 2025 Americans spent over 6.5 billion hours on tax preparation. Ninety percent of the tax returns had to be prepared by hired professionals. Between the costs of the IRS for enforcement and the time spent on taxpayers doing returns, it was costing over $400 billion each year to the US economy. And remember all the ads on TV or radio pitching negotiation services for people behind on their taxes with the IRS? What a broken system that was! We didn't want to repeat that mistake.

"We don't tax sales or transfers of goods or services between companies. That would be a hidden tax and would not meet our transparency requirement. We also don't tax spending money on capital investment. So if a rich person buys a yacht for a million Midas, we would tax it at 9 percent, but if he or she built a plant making widgets for a million Midas, there would be no tax.

"Our major source of taxes is the property tax. But our property tax is different from the system typically used in the US. In the US, the tax is a percentage of the total value of the property. So if the owner builds a structure or improves his property, then his taxes go up. We don't think that is right. What additional benefit has the government given to the property owner to justify the additional tax? Where does the government offer the value proposition we talked about in exchange for the tax? What additional cost has the government borne as a result of the improvement? The government might argue the costs of police and fire protection have risen as the size of the building has increased, but that is a weak connection. The major increases in costs are borne by the insurance companies that insure the buildings against fire or other losses, and those costs are directly passed on to the property owner in the form of insurance premiums."

"So what is your property tax system, if not based on value?"

"We base it on the value contributed by the government, not by the property owner. And that value is the land on which the building is placed, not the building itself."

Joe was perplexed. "You mean you only tax the raw land value? What the owner builds on it is untaxed?"

"Exactly. If the government provides good services in the way of police and fire protection, keeps crime low, allows good schools to flourish, develops master plans in a rational and pleasing way, provides good transportation, promotes liberty and unlimited opportunity, is free of corruption, and has reasonable spending and taxes, then people will want to live here. If the demand to be here is high, prices go up and stay up. So that's the wealth the government has created for the private resident and property owner, and that's what gets taxed. What the property owner does for himself by building from scratch or constructing an improvement, that is not taxed."

Joe was scratching his head as he mulled over what Darin had said. It just seemed to make too much sense.

"But how do you determine what the land value is and split that off? In the typical system, when a property sells, don't you have hard evidence of the total value but not of the portions attributed to the land and to the buildings?"

"Good question. In the old tax system, the assessor would value a property based on its recent sales price, or in the case where that particular piece had not sold recently, then comparable properties would be used to estimate value. So the vast majority of properties are taxed on estimates of value, not on actual numbers. My point here is that even the old system, supposedly based on hard numbers, is far from perfect and is based on a rough estimation. So we are not expecting perfection in our system, either, just striving for more accuracy.

"Remember, we originally bought the island from Detroit for $1 billion, about $1 million an acre. That money was raised by a consortium of private investors. In addition to the land purchase, money was raised for the various costs of planning and the interest carry on the original investment. The investors were promised a preferred return and expected to be paid back over a thirty-year period. The investors were also given first opportunities to buy land for their office centers they intended to build on Belle Isle. That was part of the deal. But the clincher, and what really excited the Wall Street crowd, was the promise that their managers and investment bankers would be guaranteed residency."

"Why was that important to them?"

"Well, remember, they were mostly New York or New Jersey residents, some from California. These were all high-tax states, and we had already established in our constitution that there would be no income taxes. Not all wanted to move, but many did. So we had our first 'customers' lined up, even before we opened our doors."

The main courses were served, and the conversation moved from Belle Isle to reminiscing about their high school days. Joe played football for Country Day, while Darin skied. Darin kept in touch with a number of their old classmates who had remained in the area and brought Joe up to date on what they were doing. Joe listened with intense interest.

He missed those days. The conversation resumed on Belle Isle.

"Joe, you asked about the property tax question. It was easy to start to value the land, as Belle Isle was basically vacant, so whatever was paid for it was totally attributed to the actions of the government. We had established our constitution, form of government, tax system, and so forth. We also had master planned the island into the various zones of office, commercial/retail, schools, and residential. But we were also careful to let the zones mix. So often, in the middle of an area that was predominantly residential, there would be a coffee shop or a produce market. Even though we're proud of our monorail, we know people like to walk.

"We set prices on each area according to its use and location. The river views commanded higher prices. Where we allowed taller buildings, the prices were higher. You get the idea.

"Then as the land sales proceeded, we adjusted our prices to meet the market. Some of our tracts sold faster than expected, so we increased the prices on those areas. On those that sold slowly, we lowered the prices. So we had real pricing information on which to base our land values for property tax purposes. And when we increased or lowered prices based on a sale, then all the similar properties' land values were adjusted accordingly. Basically the same comparable sales system used on the old system, but we applied it on a land-value-only basis."

"But, Darin, once all the land is taken and you don't have any vacant land sales, then what do you use for land value?"

"Joe, when a sale takes place, we basically subtract the value of the building and improvements from the sale price and take the remainder as the land value. The assessor uses tables to calculate the depreciated value of the building.

"For example, let's say you bought a lot for 200,000 Midas and built a house on it for 800,000 Midas. Your total cost, including the land, is 1,000,000. You pay taxes only on the 200,000 initially. Seven years later, you sell the house and lot to a new buyer for 1,200,000. The house is seven years old now, and let's say you haven't put any improvements into the house, only maintained it. We estimate the house alone has depreciated 10 percent in value, from our studies of house values over the last one hundred years. So now your house by itself is worth the original cost of 800,000 less 10 percent, or about 720,000. So the land is the balance, and 1,200,000 less 720,000 equals 480,000. So the land value has increased from 200,000 to 480,000 over the seven-year period. The new buyer would pay taxes on 480,000, but also all owners of similarly sized lots would see their assessed land values adjusted accordingly. But keep in mind this transaction would be one of many, and all the transactions would be considered and averaged out.

"Also, that doesn't mean the buyer's taxes would go up that much, if at all. Because the taxes are based on how much we spend on government, not how much we *could* take in. In fact, the taxes may go down, depending on what is happening on other types of real estate. We automatically adjust the rate each year based on the total assessed value and the annual spending budget. And remember, if the government isn't doing a good job, there would be *no* increase in land value. When a property owner sees a real increase in value, they are happy, believe me."

"How about if the homeowner makes improvements during that seven-year period—let's say an addition?"

"Then we increase the building value by our estimate of what was spent on the improvements and apply the depreciation schedule separately to that improvement. That way, there is no increase in land value due to what was spent on the improvements. We have similar schedules for remodeling.

"On commercial properties, we use the same approach. Businesses depreciate in real value also. Buyer preferences change, and buildings become obsolete. In the case of this class of commercial buildings, the figure is about 2 percent per year. So let's say in the case of Andrew's restaurant, he sells it after a ten-year hold for what he paid for it. The building value is now 20 percent less, and the land has increased by the same dollar amount. What caused the land to increase in value? For a restaurateur, it increased because the government did a great job in attracting new residents who are his customers, for providing clean, safe, and heated streets and good transportation to move customers to his restaurant. We are not making adjustments without information. When a business changes hands, then we have a 'comp,' which we apply, in conjunction with other sales, to all similar properties."

Joe's head was swimming with figures.

"Darin, you said the land value went up because the government did a great job. Who determines if they are truly doing a great job?"

"Great question. The market determines. Every time a customer walks in the door here, it is a 'yes' vote for the great job being done."

"But it seems to me Andrew could argue that his great food and service caused the value to go up, not something the government did."

"I'm sure Andrew would argue that, and if you remember my brother, he's not shy about engaging in argument. But remember, we are valuing classes of property *equally*, with a number of data points, not just off one transaction. So Andrew's hypothetical sale would be just one data point in all the sales in the Restaurant/Entertainment

District. Also, if his restaurant increases in sales and profits over time, at least *some* of the effect is due to the fact people want to come to the district to eat and shop and so forth. Our part in that is to provide a safe, pleasing street environment. The basic principle here is you pay us for what we do for you and don't pay us for what you do for yourself."

Joe reflected on their discussion about property taxes. He had a recent experience in Bratislava that was relevant. His company had experienced strong growth in the biotech field, needed more space, and had built a new corporate headquarters with company funds, far larger than the former. The new property tax bill was five times what they had been previously paying and much more than expected. This had all kinds of downstream effects. The hit on their income statement caused their lender to cut their credit line considerably, which forced them to cancel a large project for one of their best customers. The customer moved their business elsewhere.

A solidly built man approached their table with a wide smile. Joe immediately recognized Darin's brother, Andrew. Four years older than Darin, Andrew, like his brother, looked younger than his age. Joe rose to his feet, and they exchanged a hug.

"Joe, it's been forever but so good to see you." Andrew grinned. "Welcome to my humble *maison*."

"Humble, hardly!" Joe retorted with a big smile. "It's beautiful, but I appreciate the attempt at modesty."

"Actually, I can't take much credit. Darin's Belle Isle Planning Department had a heavy hand on the exterior design—man, what a pain in the butt they were! Although I have to say, in the end it worked out well."

Darin answered more for Joe's benefit. "What Andrew is referring to is the control the planning department has over the architecture. Now many cities have planning commissions and architectural review boards, but they are composed of people who are either elected or appointed by elected officials. Here on Belle Isle, we answer to our investors, whose goal is to maximize the value of the island. So the NIMBYs aren't running the show.

"What's a NIMBY?"

"Sorry, it's a term all of us in real estate development know all too well—not in my backyard."

Andrew joined them at their table, and they continued talking about the old days at Country Day. After dinner, Andrew ordered a twenty-year-old tawny port, as did Darin. Joe had a cappuccino.

"Well, I'm going to get back to work." Andrew got up to leave. "Dinner is on the house tonight. And enjoy your stay."

They embraced one more time, and Andrew disappeared.

Back on the monorail, Joe marveled at the views as they sped around the island. The sun had just set, and the buildings were bathed in the warm glow of the streetlights. As the monorail turned to the west, the Detroit Yacht Club passed below to their right. Past the yacht club was the beach. Three young couples were sitting on the sand around a firepit ablaze with burning logs. Up ahead, Joe could see the twin towers of the Four Seasons, with its blue lights running up its sides. Joe took a picture with his phone but knew it wouldn't match the reality. A few minutes later, they were back at the Four Seasons. They decided to meet at ten o'clock the next morning, and Joe exited through the monorail's doors.

Chapter 7

DAY TWO

The secret to happiness in life is
to have more and want less.
—Dr. Harry Harding

Joe was a few minutes late as he entered the coffee shop off the lobby of the Four Seasons. Darin was seated at a table in the corner, busy on his smartphone, apparently on a videoconference call with earbuds in and a low-volume mike. He looked up, motioned for Joe to have a seat, and quickly finished his call.

"Good morning. How'd you sleep?"

"Great. I feel like a new man. And the communication center in the room worked great."

"Good to hear. So Bratislava is still standing?"

"Yes, sir. Sometimes I feel like they would rather not have me around. I get in the way."

"I know the feeling, but it's a good one. It means you've trained your staff well."

"I hope so. By the way, what is behind the name 'von Mises Suite'?"

Darin answered, "Oh, von Mises. He was an economist from the Austrian school of economics. His full name is Ludwig von Mises.

He was born in the late 1800s in Austria-Hungary. Being Jewish, he fled Europe at the start of World War II and settled in New York City. He taught at NYU and wrote that socialism must fail because it had no pricing system, and prices are absolutely needed to allocate resources to what people want. That's the short version of a complex economic theory. Von Mises influenced many people, including the novelist Ayn Rand."

"So is the painting in the room von Mises?"

"Yes, it is." Darin continued, "We always try to name important things after people who espoused our core principles. So we have rooms named after free-market economists and novelists like Ayn Rand and some buildings after famous architects and some of our streets and parks after leaders of our founding group. But one thing you will never see is anything named after an elected official."

The waitress brought Turkish coffee and an assortment of Danish pastries and fruit.

"So, Darin, what's on the agenda today? I hope I'm not getting in the way of your work."

"Not at all. I have the day-to-day done by others. My time is blocked off for you. This morning we are touring the Service Center, and after lunch we're going over to the Business District to tour one of the investment firms. If we have time, we'll stop by Andrew's office. I have some nap time for you later in the afternoon, and then we're having dinner at my place. I've invited a few friends to join us. They want to meet you."

The weather was warm with a light breeze, so they walked to the Service Center, which was less than a mile to the east. They walked in the middle of the street, as did others, although Joe noted there were sidewalks on both sides. Joe hadn't seen a car, only people on foot, some bicycles, and an occasional minivehicle, which resembled a golf cart, with four seats and a sunroof.

Chapter 8

STREET DESIGN

The truth has no agenda.

—General George Patton

"Darin, are cars not allowed on Belle Isle? It's so quiet compared to Bratislava!"

"Actually cars are allowed on Belle Isle, but only a few times a year, and they have to be race cars," Darin answered with a smile.

"Many of our residents have cars, but they keep them at the Transportation Center on the other side of the river and use the monorail to access them."

"Then why do you have a street rather than a wide pedestrian sidewalk?"

"Two reasons. As I mentioned, we spent a lot of time on the master planning for Belle Isle. We studied other city-states for ideas, and one we looked at closely was Monaco. Monaco is one-half the size of Belle Isle—they have less than twenty-two million square feet of land area, and we have almost forty-three million. Their population is thirty-three thousand, and ours is designed up to fifty thousand, so our population density is less than theirs. We have some opportunities for a little more open space, and we use it, as you will see. But one of our early objectives was to put Belle Isle on the world map, particularly as we wanted to attract international investment firms to put their North American headquarters here. So cultural issues matter to us, and we thought that having world-class racing events here would appeal to the younger crowd, who are the movers and shakers. Competition is contagious.

"So our primary street is basically designed as a racecourse, with some straightaways, turns, an esse, a chicane, and the whole bit. We hired a team of prominent Formula 1 track architects to consult on the design. It's worked out well, and our race weeks here are the highlights of the off-winter seasons.

"We also have secondary streets, but they are narrower, just wide enough for service vehicles to deliver fresh produce, pick up the trash, and deliver building materials and construction equipment and for fire trucks, ambulances, and so forth. But the nonemergency vehicles are only allowed to travel on the streets from 3:00 a.m. to 7:00 a.m. And we have severe noise restrictions, so they are very quiet. Of course emergency vehicles are allowed at any time and have sirens to warn people off the streets.

"The other vehicles allowed deal with snow removal, but they aren't needed generally in high-pedestrian-traffic areas, such as the Shopping/Entertainment District, because the streets and sidewalks are heated in those areas."

"Isn't that expensive?"

"Not really. We use the heated residual water from the nuclear electric plant, which is basically free. It runs through pipes buried beneath the streets and walks."

"Darin, in Bratislava, we have a lot of concrete walks, streets, and buildings. I haven't seen any concrete here. What gives?"

"Concrete doesn't meet our aesthetic test. So we only allow very limited use of any that is visible. If it is used for structural reasons, it has to have an exterior material added to hide it, or if in small amounts, we allow it to be tinted. You notice the street is made of asphalt, which is actually to Formula 1 specs. The sidewalks are composed of many different materials that complement and integrate with the facades of the buildings they serve. When a property owner submits architectural plans for their building, they also submit the sidewalk materials that are proposed to use. So you notice, as we are walking here, the sidewalks are changing with the buildings. Some brick pavers, some slate, different stones. Right now we're walking on smooth cobbles. We only require that they look good, meet smoothness standards, and of course are wide enough. It's an approach Carmel, California, uses."

"It looks great! Much more interesting than a concrete sidewalk that I'm used to seeing."

"Thanks! One could say our concrete prohibition is a sort of a political statement. In the Soviet era, the Russians built the ugliest buildings in the world using primarily concrete. Concrete was cheap, and the Soviet economy couldn't afford more. Not here! In our free-market world, we go the other direction. We value beauty. I also might add, we can afford it."

"Yes, I know what you mean. In Bratislava we have the historic district, built many centuries ago, which is beautiful. Then in the newer outlying areas, such as Podvornice, built during the Soviet era, the housing is all high-rise concrete buildings, with little fenestration and no visual appeal. I actually feel depressed when I'm out there."

Chapter 9

RESIDENCY

Progress starts with the truth.
—Dan Sullivan

They were interrupted by a siren. Joe looked up and saw an ambulance coming down the street, heading toward the bridge to the mainland. Pedestrians were clearing the street to make a path and stopped and watched. Most of them were clapping, and a few were cheering. Attached to the top of the ambulance was a pink balloon. Joe looked at Darin. "What's happening?"

Darin replied, "A woman is having a baby, and they're probably heading to the Detroit Medical Center or perhaps Henry Ford Hospital. Many of our deliveries take place off the island. If the ambulance operator knows ahead of time what the sex of the baby is, they tie a balloon with the appropriate color. If not, they do a blue and a pink. The people on the street are clapping because they know soon we are going to have another Belle Islander among us."

Joe asked, "You say another Belle Islander, but this baby will be born in the US and therefore will be a US citizen, right?"

"Well, in our arrangements with the US, Belle Isle residency is based on having a resident parent. If a person is born on the island, that does not automatically entitle them to be a Belle Isle resident. They must have a parent who is. It's modeled after the system used by most European nations. Of course we also have a naturalization process. All our original residents were 'naturalized,' as are the current immigrants."

"How does someone become a resident, if not born into it?"

"They apply to our Residency Board. The Residency Board is composed of three members who review applications. During busy times we have more than one board going. The majority of our applications come from the US, but we have many also from France and Great Britain, some from Canada, and quite a few from Central and South America, even Asia."

"What are the requirements?"

"Well, first of all, they can't be a criminal escaping from somewhere. Also, they have to have paid their bills and have good credit. That applies to everyone. Then most prospects have to make a substantial contribution of capital, either directly to the Belle Isle Treasury or to a business based on Belle Isle."

"What kind of contribution are we talking about?"

"For a direct contribution, it's several hundred thousand Midas. I don't recall the exact number today. For a business, it's higher."

"That seems like a lot."

"It is, but remember, we paid a big sum to buy the island from Detroit, then we had to put in the infrastructure—the roads, the monorail, utilities, and so forth. We did this by raising money with bonds that are repaid from the residency fees. We also have purchased commodities that back up the Midas with those fees. And keep in mind, we have more applications than we have openings."

"But it seems to me you end up with only rich people. It sounds pretty exclusionary."

"Not really. Early on we worked with several of the banks on a loan program for aspiring residents. The resident would pay a percentage of the total fee, like 10 to 20 percent, and then repay the balance over the years from their income tax savings. Sort of like a home mortgage arrangement.

"Also we hold 20 percent of our residency spots open for 'exceptions.' These are people who cannot afford the standard contribution and can't qualify for the bank loan but have some other attribute that we think will benefit Belle Isle. So we have 'starving artists,' some talented musicians, some teachers with special knowledge. For example, we had an application a few years back from an Italian gentleman who was a master stonecutter in Italy. He had read about some of our architectural goals here and wrote to say he wanted to help. He is now teaching his craft to others on the island at one of our trade schools. As you walk around the island, you'll see some of his work. It's just amazing. He didn't have the standard contribution but came anyway."

Darin continued, "And we have some people who came here with absolutely nothing. Nothing but a burning desire to take advantage of the unlimited opportunity that Belle Isle offers. People who ask for nothing but a chance to make a better life for themselves and their family. You'll meet one of them at my home tonight over dinner, Hector Cabrera. Hector was from Mexico. Came here dirt poor. Great story.

"Another group of people who apply are the entrepreneurs. Many are from other continents who have businesses that are either being hugely overtaxed or are in danger of being nationalized. They know there are no business taxes and absolutely no risk of the government getting into their business. Did I tell you, Belle Isle is ranked number one in the world in terms of business climate and political risk? These entrepreneurs come here with plans and expertise, often little else. They meet with the financial types who are based here, raise their capital, and start or continue their businesses. Often they take office space for their administrative and engineering functions but then look for industrial land to build factories. We have very little industrial land on the island because we don't have the room, so the factories are getting built across the river in Detroit. They want their manufacturing plants to be close where they can be supervised, not in China or somewhere far away. In fact, many of these folks *are* from China. They left China because the government was in their faces. One of our biggest success stories is a Chinese family that makes retinal-activated screens for smartphones—they engineer on Belle Isle, build in Detroit, and ship all over the world.

"So quite a bit of the abandoned land in old Detroit is now becoming industrial parks with brand-new buildings and so forth. These new plants employ a lot of people from Detroit. And Detroit and Southeast Michigan have come roaring back with all the investment."

Joe stroked his chin. It was a subconscious action on his part when he was deep in thought. He knew Belle Isle wasn't a one-off, as he had visited Hong Kong, Singapore, and Shenzhen and seen for himself what tremendous growth looked like. It was like a reservoir held back by massive gates, suddenly opened to release a surge of water. He guessed that Detroit would be able to transform just as much as those other cities.

Chapter 10

SERVICE CENTER I

Government is not reason; it is not eloquence. It is force.
And force, like fire, is a dangerous servant and a fearful master.
—George Washington

The Service Center loomed on their left. It was a three-story building largely made of stucco and stone. Brick pavers welcomed visitors to the large doors. Above the portico were the words "Belle Isle Service Center."

Darin noticed Joe's gaze at the entry.

"We don't call it the government building. We use the term 'Service Center.' Words are powerful, and we try to use simple words and phrases to set the tone of our mission, which is to serve our residents, to work for them. We try to reinforce that at every opportunity. One of the trends in the US had been the advent of the 'ruling class,' often called the elites. People resented it, and the government's approval rating remained abysmal. We try to go in the other direction, having a bottom-up government rather than a top-down one."

He continued as they entered the building. "Here we have police, fire, administration, courts, and the jail. Administration includes assessment and taxes, records, planning and building, and charitable support. I have my office here."

They took the elevator up to the third floor, entered through a door marked "Administration," and continued down a hallway to an area designated as "Planning and Building." Past a reception desk was an open area with work cubicles, separated by movable partitions. Joe counted four people in front of computer screens. To the left was a large conference room with various plans and renderings adorning the walls. On the right were some doors leading to offices. Darin led Joe into one of them. To the right of the door was a small sign that simply read, "Darin Fraser." There was no job title or position described.

Joe was surprised at how small Darin's office was. For someone as famous as Darin had become and the guiding force behind such a successful city, Joe expected a more grandiose office. It couldn't have been more than twelve by fifteen feet and had a single desk with a monitor and two guest chairs. A window looked out to the south, but the view of the river was blocked by the backs of various high-rise buildings. A schefflera plant was in the corner near the window, soaking up the morning sun. Darin grabbed two waters from a small refrigerator, handed one to Joe, sat down behind his desk, and motioned for Joe to sit in the facing guest chair.

Darin recognized the look of bewilderment on Joe's face. He'd seen it many times before.

"Yeah, I know it's small. Remember, I'm a servant of the people. I work for them. I'm spending their money. So they have the best views from their homes or apartments, the nicest offices if they choose to pay for them. I actually have everything I need here to do my job. Notice the video camera feeds. I can hook up here with the best consultants in the world with a few keystrokes on the computer and talk to them in person. It works very well. It's all I need."

Joe reflected, "Darin, now that you mention it, I have often wondered about most of the government buildings I have seen. They are typically large, ornate, and expensive. And this is all over the world. I wonder if they are designed to show beauty or power. Or both? Modesty doesn't seem part of the equation."

Chapter 11

CULTURE AND RECREATION

There are obviously two educations. One should teach us how to make a living and the other how to live.
—James Truslow Adams

There was a large monitor on the wall opposite the window. Darin punched a few keys on his computer, and a slideshow started. It ran about eight minutes and talked about the recent history of Belle Isle, the mission of the community, and the philosophies and approaches used in the planning and design. Being ranked number one in the world for business climate and political risk was mentioned more than once. Darin's voice moderated the show, and at the end, he appeared on the roof of the Four Seasons, giving his closing remarks. It was well done.

"We use this as our puff piece when drumming up interest for businesses that are considering locating here. Of course quality of life is very important, so that's why we emphasize our schools and recreation, the boating, and the cultural events, both here and across the river in Detroit. We talk about the history of Belle Isle and how we have refurbished the Belle Isle Aquarium, which is the oldest aquarium in the United States. We value history and have saved and fixed up many of the historical structures, including the Casino, the Nancy Brown Peace Carillon tower, among others.

"We also have some great tourist and entertainment events going on all year. I already mentioned the Formula 1 race. The race is in June, and all the restaurants and hotels are absolutely packed. Many of the restaurants along the racecourse have outdoor sundecks that make for popular viewing spots. The international reporters give us a lot of press all over the world. It's good for business.

"Say, I'd like you to meet the lady who puts this all together."

Darin picked up his phone.

"Marta, do you have a minute? Yes, I'm in my office."

Shortly, a woman in her early fifties with wavy, shoulder-length dark-brown hair streaked with silver appeared. She wore a crisp white blouse under a burgundy blazer showing the Belle Isle logo on the left lapel. Charcoal-gray trousers and black leather flats completed her attire. She carried a small notebook and pen, ready to take notes if needed.

"Marta, please meet my good friend Joe Sharif. He is here visiting from Slovakia. Joe, Marta Lopez is our events director and is responsible for making Belle Isle the spot to be. She is originally from Barcelona but has been here over ten years. Marta, run down for Joe some of our activities."

Marta tapped her notebook as she thought about where to begin.

"Well, in July we have the Thunderbolt hydroplane races, which are a Detroit River tradition and very popular and going on right now. The racecourse runs from the Belle Isle bridge past the Detroit Yacht Club. The favorite spots to watch it are the yacht club and Belle Isle Beach.

"In August we have the Red Bull air races, where the aerobatic racers fly around pylons just to our west. Red Bull has been a sponsor here for over five years, and we're happy to have them.

"In September we have our Creation Day 5K/10K races. We still celebrate the US's July Fourth with fireworks and the like, but we also celebrate our own Creation Day, which is September fourteenth. So we have a race that day, and it attracts all kinds of runners, both Belle Islanders and Detroiters. Some runners and their friends even come in from Chicago. In early October we have the Detroit Free Press Marathon, which runs through Detroit, Windsor, and Belle Isle."

Joe cut in, "You guys like races, don't you?"

Darin answered, "No, we *love* races. Gets the adrenaline going and reflects the competitive spirit of Belle Isle."

Marta continued, "Also in October we have Halloween, of course, and have a lot of fun doing it. It's become a tradition for shopkeepers and restaurant staff to dress up in costumes. They do their normal business but also encourage young trick-or-treaters to come in and grab special treats on their walk around the island."

Marta could see Joe's interest by his raised eyebrows.

"In December, on the evening of the twenty-third, informal groups of carolers tour the downtown and sing Christmas carols outside the shops and restaurants. It's a big festival night, and most restaurants are serving on the outside sundecks that night. People are dressed in their winter clothes, eating whatever and drinking schnapps while being serenaded. I'm not sure who has more fun that evening—the carolers or the carolees!

"But the most fun event of the year is the Winterfest. We don't have the international crowd the Formula 1 race attracts, but it's a very lively group. We hold it at the end of January, when the weather is the coldest. It's a three-day event starting on a Friday afternoon and ending on Sunday. Friday evening we have an outdoor hockey game featuring two of the top college hockey teams in the US. We play it at the football field in the Sports Complex. We only have seating for ten thousand people, so tickets are hard to get, and we are sold out years ahead.

"In Parc de Leon, our park near downtown, we have the ice sculpture festival. One of our sponsors is UBS. They donate 25,000 Midas in prize money, so some of the best ice sculptors from around the world come in for it. It is absolutely amazing what they can do. Last year someone carved Belle Isle itself, with a lot of architectural detail!

"But the highlight of the Winterfest, in my opinion, is the Sled Dog Marathon. It is so much fun! It starts on Saturday at 9:00 p.m. and runs all night along the racecourse right through downtown and around the island. In preparation for it, we shut down the street heating system a week ahead and truck in and spread snow on the course if we need to. The dogs run all night and finish up twelve hours later. Whoever has run the farthest is the winner. Again, there is significant donor support and prize money, so teams come from Alaska and the Yukon. We set up temporary dog shelters in one of the parks for the dogs. This event is so popular, the restaurants and bars stay open all night as the fans cheer on their favorites. The drivers and dogs come into town about a week early, so by race time, many of the Islanders have come to know them personally, and they cheer loudly for their favorites, and a lot of wagering takes place!"

Darin cut in, "Many Michigan people complain about the winters here and have places in Florida. In my opinion they're missing out on the experience of the four distinct seasons. Let's take advantage of them: fall colors, winter snow, spring flowers, warm summers."

WELCOME TO
SINGAPORE
BELLE ISLE

Chapter 12

DETROIT

Status quo, you know, is Latin for "the mess we're in."

—Ronald Reagan

Darin continued, "Also, as you notice, we talk about Detroit and what it has to offer in the way of theater, arts, restaurants, entertainment, and, of course, sports. Detroit is a very important part of our promotion of the island. And it's quite accessible. You can get door-to-door to downtown in about twenty minutes from Belle Isle."

"So how is Detroit doing? When I left, it was really in a bad way."

"It's gone through a lot of change. From 1950 to 2025, Detroit lost a tremendous amount of population, going from almost 1,900,000 to about 625,000 people."

"How did Detroit turn itself around?" Joe asked.

"It wasn't easy. There were so many problems. High crime, high spending, poor city services, all made worse by extremely low population density. Detroit had 5,000 people per square mile, Chicago had 12,000, Manhattan 70,000.

"The public unions fought any attempts at real reform. There were agreements made between the city and the state to make changes, but these agreements were soon violated. Nothing seemed to work.

Finally the inevitable happened."

"What was that?"

"Well, you remember Detroit went bankrupt about 2015. After it came out of bankruptcy, it had a clean balance sheet but still suffered serious operating budget issues caused by a low tax base. The downtown area was revitalized with the help of Dan Gilbert and the Ilitch family, but high property taxes stifled new development in other areas. So the city and state put together a plan to decentralize Detroit and replace the old system with a collection of smaller political jurisdictions, sort of like New York and London. They also are called boroughs. Each of the boroughs was chosen based on its neighborhood identity and the fact it had property values that could support services. So now we have the boroughs of Palmer Woods, East Village, Jefferson, Corktown, Midtown, Woodbridge, Mexican Village, among others. Detroit's former downtown area is now its own borough with the name Detroit. It has the sports stadiums, theaters, restaurants, offices, and some residential. Detroit has about 45,000 people within its borough limits, but the overall area is still known as Greater Detroit, and its population has grown significantly.

"These new boroughs have their own governments and taxation rates. They are now much more accountable than under the old system. And they have a population density that can support these services efficiently. Without population density, it is impossible to have great services.

"Many areas of old Detroit that did not become part of the heavily populated districts were turned into urban farms, forests, and parks. They're called green zones. The billion dollars that were received from the sale of Belle Isle helped fund the relocation of residents from green zones to the populated areas.

"The plan was put together with the help of urban planning experts and endorsed by the state. It was quickly approved. Then positive changes started to happen, and they happened rather quickly."

Joe asked, "Tell me more about the new Detroit. You say people have moved back?"

"Yes. Many are younger professionals who live in lofts and rehabbed buildings. They come from all ethnicities, attracted by the culture, so Detroit is now an integrated city. I've talked a lot to these so-called urban pioneers and have gotten a good feel for what has attracted them to Detroit. They speak of the great old buildings in the city. Detroit has some of the coolest architecture that is found only in cities like New York or Chicago. Detroit borders Canada, which gives it an international flavor. The Detroit River and the surrounding connected lakes make Detroit both a major shipping and commerce link and offer lots of recreation opportunities. And the city has an artistic bohemian culture, which, combined with its music culture, makes it a cool place to be. Some attribute the spark that revitalized Detroit to the hip bars of that era like the Cafe D'Mongo's Speakeasy. Young people loved those places. And when they married and had kids, many stayed because there were, and are now, many good private and public schools. What turned the corner for these communities was having their own governments. The crime, bad schools, high taxes, and corruption of the old Detroit killed it. The boroughs that replaced old Detroit are much more efficient and accountable. Once that happened, people started moving back."

Joe reflected, "Before I left, I recall the downtown area of Detroit had made quite a turnaround, but the other areas seemed to have been left behind. But now the way you describe it, there is a coalescence that solves the problem of population density, or I guess lack of it. But doesn't the core of Detroit make it happen?"

"Absolutely. We need Detroit. Detroit's the cultural anchor for the area, including Belle Isle. It's one of the few cities on the continent that has a major league team in every sport—baseball, football, basketball, and hockey. Plus a world-class art museum, opera house, symphony, and theaters.

"But Detroit needs Belle Isle too. First of all, our residents comprise a major donor base to these institutions. But more importantly Belle Isle's reputation, which is now worldwide, has attracted tremendous investment to the area. High-tech manufacturing has added thousands of jobs on the Detroit side of the river. There are businesses headquartered on Belle Isle, but they manufacture in Detroit. Have you heard of the Siccatta watch?"

"I think so. Is that the watch that listens, talks, can read your eyes, and do all sorts of things? Sort of a watch/smartphone combination? I think they are selling some in Slovakia now."

"Yes, that's it. Well, they are all made here in Detroit by Shinola. Detroit may become the new Switzerland!

"Also, Detroiters have largely built Belle Isle. We've created thousands upon thousands of new jobs, particularly for the construction industry, as we built the new hotels, restaurants, schools, churches, homes, the monorail—you name it. Everything from scratch. During the construction heyday, our national tree was the construction crane! And now we have all kinds of permanent jobs, many of which are filled by Detroiters."

Darin continued, "And back on the Detroit side of the river, the farming that is done in the green zones is very interesting. As society has moved to healthier organic foods, the trend has been to grow healthy strains of various fruits, vegetables, and even meat products.

Flowers have become big too. We grow them year-round with special greenhouses. This doesn't lend itself to the mass-farming methods used in Iowa and other farming states that have large tracts of land. It requires more handwork and personal attention.

"I think I mentioned to you my brother, Andrew, grows specialty tomatoes. Well, that is done largely by hand on one of the Detroit farms. He employs a lot of people. Many are former prisoners who are reentering society and developing work skills. The tomatoes are shipped each morning during the harvest season to our market, along with other farmers' products. We have our own farmers market on the island, and most of the stuff is grown on the Detroit farms. Andrew also uses those tomatoes in his salsa products.

"So between the construction jobs, the new factories, and specialty farming, Detroit is coming back big-time. On the Detroit side of the bridge, a whole new community has sprung up, called Jefferson. It has all kinds of shopping, businesses, and residential. We were all surprised at how fast it happened. But I tell you, it's all about attitude. You let people see, feel, and taste unlimited opportunity—well, just step aside and get out of the way. Otherwise you get run over."

Chapter 13

SERVICE CENTER II

Be thankful we're not getting all the government we're actually paying for.
—Will Rogers

Darin and Joe finished their waters and left Darin's office to continue the tour. Passing by an office marked "Accounting," Darin stuck his head in and motioned for Joe to follow. Sitting at his desk was an older man of African descent, staring intently at his computer screen. Darin introduced Herbert Watson to Joe.

"Herbert heads our accounting department here. He makes sure everyone gets paid on time and keeps the island's books straight. Meet Joe Sharif. He came all the way from Slovakia to see us."

Herbert rose and greeted Joe with a broad smile. "We're truly honored by your visit. Darin has been talking about it for weeks. I finally get to place a face with the name."

"Well, thank you. You all have been very kind."

Darin spoke. "Herbert, I'm having Joe over for dinner at my place tonight and would like you to join us if you're free. Jessica is coming and maybe Priya Desai. Can you make it?"

"Can't, man. My wife has tickets tonight at the Fox. *Wicked* is playing. Otherwise would have loved to."

"How is Dianne? Is she still into her art?"

"Yup. Either in her studio or watching the grandkids. She's busy."

"Well, tell her I said hi, and we'll have to get together soon. Enjoy the play. I saw it last week. Loved it."

Directly next to Herbert's office was Assessments and Taxes. Upon entering the reception area, Joe was struck by the collage of pictures on the walls depicting the various activities that were done with the taxes collected. Many were Norman Rockwell paintings, such as the policeman sitting next to the runaway kid at the soda bar. Others were actual photos. One was an ambulance transporting a patient to the medical center. Another was a fireman with a soot-blackened face, shooting a stream of water from a hose at a burning house.

Darin smiled. "Here is where people come to appeal their assessments, so we figured why not do a little marketing on where their money goes to put them in a better mood?

"Also, since transparency is important to us, we post the pay schedule and job descriptions of all Service Center employees right here on this board. So the taxpayers again know where their money is going. We also post the budget for all Service Center activities."

"Don't the employees feel their privacy is a bit violated, with everyone knowing what they make?"

"At first. But now they accept it. We stress that transparency is essential in the public areas to earn the public trust. If they want to keep their pay private, they need to work in the private sector."

Walking past reception, they came to an open area with a woman working on a computer.

"Sheila is keeping the tax assessments current based on transaction data. She sends out all the new assessments each year by February 1.

Over here we have the conference and appeals room. We have appeals in the first two weeks of February. The Board of Appeals is composed of three residents who are appointed for overlapping three-year terms by the president and confirmed by the council. The Board of Appeals members are paid a nominal amount for their time."

"Do you get many appeals?"

"Oh, about ten on average, sometimes a few more. As we base the raw land value on an algorithm backed by actual data, it's pretty cut-and-dried. As I mentioned before, everyone is taxed the same based on computed land values. It's pretty hard to argue with it. But of course we take everyone's appeal seriously, and sometimes we make mistakes."

BELLE · ISLE

Chapter 14

CHARITABLE SUPPORT

Socialism, like the ancient ideas from which it springs, confuses the distinction between government and society. As a result of this, every time we object to a thing being done by government, the socialists conclude that we object to its being done at all.

—Frédéric Bastiat

The last door on the third-floor hallway was marked "Charitable Support." Like the others, it had a small reception area with walls sprinkled with photos of people helping other people. One was a man dressed like Santa Claus, with a large bag slung over his shoulder, surrounded by a small group of children. Another showed a young smiling girl holding a puppy, and next to it was a framed photo of a Salvation Army kettle with some Salvation soldiers. It was signed by a Salvation Army colonel.

"This department's mission is to support charitable work. We have virtually no government involvement in the traditional social safety net. But we believe that everyone should have adequate food, shelter, education, and health care. We just leave it to the charitable sector to supply these things for the less fortunate. What we *do* is promote and foster support for the charities that provide those things. Charities that engage in fundraising here have to register with us and provide documentation for our approval if they want to have our certification and support."

"What kind of documentation do they have to provide?"

"Well, their purpose and mission, of course. Then also their annual operating budget and audited financial statements that show all the salaries of paid staff, the number of paid staff hours and volunteer hours, what percentage of their revenue is spent on fundraising, and the like. Also, and this is very important, what key metrics have they established to measure their effectiveness? For example, for a food program, how many meals did they serve? For health-care support, how many patients were seen? And the metrics have to be audited also. What we are trying to do is to make sure that money is being raised efficiently and that the money is well spent on the intended purpose and not soaked up by excessive overhead and salaries. We actually issue ratings based on our analysis, sort of like Moody's or Standard & Poor's would do for a corporation. But because we are a small city with limited staff, we monitor and issue ratings for only about twenty charities."

"But, Darin, I guess I don't understand. In the US, charities are designated as such, which allows contributions to them to be tax deductible. But since one doesn't pay any income tax here, why does it matter? I assume people are free to give money to whomever they want. So what is the advantage to a charity to have a good rating?"

"Two reasons. First, people here are busy, and many don't have the time to carefully research the effectiveness of a charity. So they rely on us to help them in making their determination. Second, we actually allocate part of our tax revenue to direct financial support of the charities if the donations fall short. But *we* don't determine which organizations get the money. Our residents do that through an online vote. There is a website that lists all the charities, including their ratings and details. Four times a year, our residents on a particular voting day go to the website, review the data and ratings, and make a percentage allocation of their vote for their favorite charities. Think of it like the old 401(k) investments our fathers had, where they allocated 20 percent of their investment to this stock and 15 percent to that stock or bond and so forth. Well, we follow the same process here. And of course people only have one vote. And some don't vote at all."

"It sounds a little complicated."

"Not really. It's quite simple and works well."

"How much of the general budget goes to charitable support?"

"About 10 percent. And we're considering cutting it back because we have accumulated quite a surplus."

They headed to the elevator and got off on the second floor.

Chapter 15

SERVICE CENTER III

Democracy must be something more than two wolves and a sheep voting on what to have for dinner.

—James Bovard

"This is the floor where we have the courts and the jail. There are three courtrooms and housing for about twenty-five prisoners."

Darin opened one of the courtroom doors and quietly walked in, motioning for Joe to join him. They took a seat on one of the back benches. The courtroom resembled those Joe had seen in the United States, with a judge behind the bench up on a raised platform and a witness chair nearby. In front were two tables with some lawyers and a jury box set to the right. In the jury box were two men and a woman, all who appeared to be in their sixties or seventies.

The lawyers were arguing what appeared to be a medical malpractice case. Joe watched with interest. Even though it was an obstetrical case, he knew all the terms and quickly caught the gist of the case. Apparently, the plaintiff was a woman who had delivered a child who later developed epilepsy. The obstetrician was being sued as a result. The plaintiff's lawyer had just wrapped up his opening statement, and the defense attorney was now showing the medical records to the court. The jurors watched with interest, passing the logs among them as the attorney went through his arguments.

Darin whispered, "The courts have different rules here. I'll explain when we get outside."

They watched for another half hour until the court recessed for lunch.

"Let's finish the tour on the first floor, then we'll get some lunch on our own."

On the first floor were police and fire, anticorruption, the president's office, and the council chamber.

"Joe, I'll show you the council chamber. The police, fire, and president's offices are rather ordinary. I think the police force numbers twenty-five policemen and administrative support staff. We have eight trained firefighters, but only two are on duty at a time. The others have day jobs and are on call. The president has a vice president, who is really like an executive assistant, and one other staff member. Anticorruption has a staff of three, and they have fairly high security. They don't give public tours."

Darin and Joe walked through a pair of large doors into a small assembly room. There was a large, wide-seated podium area with ten seats and the names of the officials in front. A speaker's podium faced the legislators' platform. Behind the speaker's podium was audience seating for perhaps eighty people.

"The council members meet once a month. The meetings are recorded and telecast. You can pick it up on your TV on the community channel. It's organized much like a typical city hall in the US."

"Are the meetings well attended?"

"Not really. Ten people would be a big turnout. We get more at budget time. Actually many times there is nothing on the agenda, and the meeting is canceled. But sometimes we get a controversial land use issue, and the turnout is greater."

Off the first-floor lobby was a cafeteria. Darin and Joe grabbed some sandwiches and took them out the back to an outside dining area, where they were shaded from the sun by a pergola made from lattice intertwined with vines. Other Service Center workers were relaxing in the noonday sun, quietly talking among themselves. Joe was starting to feel a lull, the fatigue from his long trip and a different time zone weighing on him.

Darin noticed. "Hey, old man, you look like you're a prospect for an afternoon siesta. We'll give you a nap break after lunch. The tour can take a break."

"I'm hanging in there. Let's keep going. This is too interesting. Say, what was going on in the courtroom? You said the rules were different."

Chapter 16

COURT PROCEDURES

He who knows best knows how little he knows.
—Thomas Jefferson

"Yes, well, we were seeing a civil tort case. The same courtroom and judges hear criminal cases too. On the criminal side, the rules are pretty much the same as most states with regard to defendants' rights, rules of evidence, and so forth. But our criminal laws are somewhat simpler. And one major difference is we don't plea-bargain. Everyone is entitled to a jury trial of their peers.

"On the civil tort side, though, our rules are quite different. In technical matters we figure the common man doesn't have the training and expertise to understand and make good judgments in today's increasingly complex world. That's not a form of elitism. It's just recognizing that our world has become increasingly specialized.

"So for instance, in the trial we observed, the jury was made up of three physicians who were experts in the matter being tried. In fact, they were probably all OB-GYNs. Usually they are retired and have the time and interest to serve as jurors. Both sides have the opportunity to interview and challenge prospective jurors, so the three who actually served have been vetted by both sides. If one of the lawyers ends up rejecting all the candidates, the judge has the authority to step in and appoint them.

"Another difference with a typical US system is how lawyers get the cases. In the US, in personal injury cases, a lawyer approaches a prospective plaintiff or gets approached and tries to sign them up with a one-third contingency fee. Often the lawyers advertise to solicit cases. We think that the lawyers often get rich in the process, leaving the plaintiffs with less money than they could otherwise get or deserve, and the one-third contingency fee amounts to price fixing. So what we do is encourage aggrieved parties to put their cases out to bid. One of our rated and supported charities provides an initial screening service for cases. A person calls a phone number, gives the details of the case in a telephone interview, and that information is posted on a website for prospective plaintiffs' attorneys to bid on. They could bid a fixed fee, a one-third contingency, or any other percentage they feel is appropriate. On some potential big cases, the attorneys bid 10 percent or lower. Along with the bid, the attorneys submit their résumés and their prior trial histories with regard to similar cases and the outcomes. Then that information is transmitted back to the potential plaintiff, who makes a decision to go forward with a particular attorney or perhaps to interview several of them."

"That certainly sounds like a more open and free-market approach to litigation."

"There's more. One of the items our courts do *not* allow to be discovered is the amount of medical malpractice insurance the physician carries. We figure that the ability to pay shouldn't play into it. The case needs to be decided on its merits. Now if the physician chooses to disclose with the approval of the insurance company, then the insurance may be disclosed. Sometimes that's done, sometimes not. It varies."

Joe queried, "Is there more?"

"Yes, the loser pays the court costs and the other attorney's charges, within reason, of course. It keeps down the questionable cases."

"So how has this affected the insurance premiums the doctors pay?"

"It has reduced them greatly. Most doctors pay only one-fifth of what the premiums would be in the US, unless they have a high claim history and the insurance companies give them poor ratings."

"Darin, that sounds great. I know my father always complained about his premiums in the US, and he wasn't in a high-risk specialty."

"Yes, and the lower premiums have translated to lower pricing, as the doctors' costs are lower. And we use the same system on other technical specialties, where the average person isn't conversant enough with the issues to render a qualified opinion as a juror."

"Like what? And how do you determine which types of things are covered by this system and which are not?"

"Well, there are a number of them. One is restaurant liability in food poisoning cases. It's rather scientific with regard to the toxins and food handling procedures, so that is one of the 'technical torts.' There are a few others. But many claims are heard by lay jurors, such as slip-and-falls."

"Darin, you also mentioned the criminal laws here are simpler than the US. I can't imagine that there's much crime. Everyone seems too content for that here."

"This is something I'd especially like to brag about. There's virtually no crime on Belle Isle. This is largely because we have no poverty here. Between our strong economy and charitable safety net, people don't need to steal or rob to put food on the table. Street crime is nil because we have so many people out walking at all times, including our cops, and the lighting is good. Also, being an island with limited access gives us more security. If a crime is committed, say a break-in, then the monorail and bridge are secured, and those are the only ways off the island, except to swim or take a boat. It works. You don't have to worry about safety here."

Chapter 17

TREASURY AND BANKING

Alexander Hamilton started the US Treasury with nothing, and that was the closest our country has ever been to being even.

—Will Rogers

The sandwiches finished, the two headed back out the front of the Service Center building and walked to the east to the next structure. Red reclaimed brick walls topped with a slate roof gave it an older look. It had a small sign in front that read, "Belle Isle Treasury."

Inside it looked like a US bank. A meeting of five people was being conducted in a glass-walled room. Two people were helping customers, and several offices lined the exterior walls.

Darin pointed to the conference room. "These are the managers and accounting people who run the treasury here. Belle Isle has a treasury like most countries. We toyed with the idea initially of using the US dollar and in fact did so for our first few years, but the deficits of the US, the public debt, and the ensuing inflation were disruptive to us. When the interest on the debt exceeded the defense budget, that was a wake-up call.

"The value of our dollar-denominated assets was falling. So we decided to cut ourselves loose from the US dollar and start our own currency. As you know, it is called a Midas. We started with pictures of people influential to our philosophy on our bills—F. A. Hayek and von Mises among them.

"When we first went with our own currency, we pegged it at par with the US dollar, but our currency, unlike the dollar, has suffered no loss of value. In fact, we picked up a little, so our Midas today is equivalent in purchasing power to the 2025 US dollars. For example, a cup of specialty coffee here costs about 5 Midas, which is what it cost in the US back in 2025. Today in the US, that same cup of coffee costs $15 or more.

"We used to have a contract with a private mint to do our currency printing and coin minting, but now all transactions are done electronically with a digital currency. Another thing we have done is to back up our currency 100 percent with a basket of commodities. We initially started off with only gold. Our initial goal was to have at least 20 percent of the outstanding currency backed by gold, similar to Switzerland, but have since added other commodities to the mix—silver, copper, oil and food contract rights, and some stable foreign currencies among them. We have tried to create a mix that helps reduce the reliance on any one item. We are now nearly 100 percent backed by something of real value."

"So I could turn in a Midas for a barrel of oil?" Joe asked.

"Well, a Midas wouldn't buy you a full barrel. But you could turn in, let's say, 500 Midas, and receive in exchange a contract for delivery of about ten barrels of oil, which is fully assignable. In other words you could trade that contract for something else of value, say US dollars or a fine dinner for twenty people."

"So how did you go from partial backing to 100 percent backing of the Midas?"

"Through our land sales, running surpluses, and the requirement that new immigrant residents make a contribution of initial capital."

"So the Midas must be well accepted, backed by gold and oil and so forth."

"Absolutely. You know the saying 'It's as good as gold'? We like to say, 'It's better than gold!'" Darin smiled. Joe thought it was a bit cheesy.

Darin continued, "We have a currency board that is made up of five knowledgeable currency experts. They rotate in from the financial institutions and are appointed by the president and approved by the council. Their clear mission is to maintain integrity of transactions and to keep the Midas strong and stable."

"Are there any banks on Belle Isle?"

"Of course. We have three banks. One is a community-type bank owned by Belle Isle residents. It's called First Bank and is freestanding and located in the retail area. The other two are international—JPMorgan Chase and UBS, and they're more office-type operations in the Financial Center. The big banks handle the bulk of the international transactions."

"Do you have government insurance or oversight on your banks?"

"No. First Bank, being rather small, buys insurance from Lloyd's to protect its depositors, and Lloyd's does the oversight of the loans and books. That gives the depositors comfort. And if Lloyd's starts charging too much or isn't giving service, First Bank can shop around in the world market and find a replacement. US banks can't do that with the FDIC—poor bastards!"

LEVY & SERVENKOV
Capital Group

Chapter 18

YURI SERVENKOV

It has been said that politics is the second-oldest profession.
I have learned that it bears a striking resemblance to the first.
—Ronald Reagan

They headed outside again, boarded the monorail, and got off at the Financial Center.

The Financial Center was actually a collection of office buildings, all connected by internal walkways and skyways. The monorail platform overlooked the main atrium lobby.

The floor was a beige Trani marble with a central Portoro marble inset, upon which a large walnut-sheathed flower box was installed. The day's freshly cut arrangement of roses and daylilies filled the flower box. Brushed chrome elevator doors and trim turned the ceiling corner and transitioned into a large light fixture, suspended by chrome cables from the lobby ceiling.

Below them, people were entering and exiting through the main doors, which were secured in a fully open position. Some were dressed in summer business suits, others in casual dress, and even some in shorts. There was a faint hint of the freshness of the river in the lobby. Darin and Joe rode the escalator down to the lobby and proceeded to the elevator bank.

They got off on the forty-fourth floor and faced an imposing corporate monument sign with large gold letters laid over a travertine marble wall that read, "Levy and Servenkov Capital Group."

Darin approached the receptionist. "I'm here to meet with Mr. Servenkov. My name is Darin Fraser. He's expecting me."

"Yes, Mr. Fraser, one moment, please. Please have a seat."

To the right of the reception desk was a lobby with full-length windows overlooking the Belle Isle bridge. Beyond it, the sun sparkled off the Hudson's tower. Turning to the right, on the wall was a large video screen with a business reporter talking about the Asian stock market while a ticker scrolled below him.

"Darin, my dear friend, how are you?" A man dressed in a beige summer suit with an open collar was striding across the lobby with open arms and a large grin. He appeared to be in his midforties, was shorter than Darin by a good six inches, and was carrying an extra twenty pounds over what his doctor probably wanted.

"It has been too long, and I am so glad you have come by to visit." They hugged, then Darin introduced Joe and Yuri Servenkov, partner in Levy and Servenkov.

Yuri motioned for them to follow him, and he carded through two sets of security doors and down a long hallway. His office was impressive by any standard. Joe thought it must be thirty by forty feet, a corner office with two window views. One view was of the villages of Detroit, surrounded by small tracts of parks and many well-cultivated farms and greenhouses. The other view was the river to the west, dominated by the Hudson's tower and the two bridges connecting the United States and Canada. Yuri's desk faced away from the views. It focused on an array of video screens; Joe counted eight, which had various stock and investment programs running. Behind Yuri's desk was a credenza with a collection of photos of Yuri with various people, most of them well known. Joe recognized four US presidents, a Russian prime minister, and a number of European heads of state. He didn't see any family photos, and Joe speculated Yuri was unmarried.

On the far side of the office was a conference table, with seating for ten. Decorating the walls were pictures of various investments the firm had made. They were quite varied. Some office buildings, a residential community the size of a small city, and a research park filled the smaller wall, which seemed dedicated to real estate. On the longer wall, pictures of public utilities dominated. Pictures of several micronuclear electric power plants, a water treatment plant, and a large number of microsewage treatment plants were framed. Joe noted the Belle Isle utilities were among them, photographed from the air with the distinctive river in the background.

The three of them sat at the conference table as an assistant brought glasses of Italian sparkling water with limes.

Yuri opened. "So, Darin, I understand from your message your friend Joe is here from Slovakia to learn more about our wonderful island. What can I show Joe today?"

Darin responded, "Yuri, I'm sure Joe would like a tour of your offices, but more importantly I think he would be interested in learning more about you and your business and why you located it here on Belle Isle."

Yuri smiled at Joe. "You have a good amount of time? The story is not short!"

Joe interjected, "Yuri, the chairs are comfortable, the drinks are cold, the view is great. I couldn't ask for a better place to hear a long story. But I am still suffering from jet lag, so forgive me if at times I listen while examining my eyelids."

"Well, Mr. Joe, I will just have to make it both interesting and short. My parents were born in Russia and came to this country before I was born. My father was a doctor in Russia but became very frustrated with the medical system there—it was still a throwback to the Soviet system and didn't reward their doctors very well. They settled near New York City, and my father established a practice. I went to NYU and got a degree in political science and then an MBA from Harvard. After graduation, I looked for job opportunities in the business and investment fields and researched carefully where the best business environments might be. New York, of course, has historically been the financial and business center for the US, and I was right there. But its tax rates and living costs were very high, and it seemed to have lost some of its entrepreneurial zeal. I even researched Michigan, but even though Michigan's taxes weren't bad, its regulatory environment inhibited doing anything creative, so I scratched it from my list too. But one thing did pop out of my Michigan investigation that directly affected my career path.

"Through a friend of my father, I arranged a meeting with the managing partner of a large venture capital fund in Michigan, just to pick his brain and get advice on what I should do with my life. He was helpful, and in the course of our discussion, he told me an interesting story. His investment fund had taken a large position in an aerospace firm based in Phoenix, Arizona, and he was given a seat on the board of directors of this company.

"Well, this Michigan person, the new board member, was attending a quarterly board meeting in Phoenix, and the management was giving their status report to the board. I guess it wasn't a good picture. The company was behind in its deliveries. It was having trouble hiring enough skilled tradespeople such as tool and die workers, machinists, precision welders, and engineers to meet its requirements. Well, our Michigan investor raised his hand and said, 'Pardon me, Mr. Chairman, but I suggest we look at opening a plant in Southeastern Michigan. The Detroit area has an abundance of those talents, as the auto industry has significantly downsized, and skilled people are looking for work.' The chairman removed his glasses and, after a long pause, looked our Michigan guy in the face and declared, 'Michigan! The home of the communist UAW? You've got to be kidding. The business climate in Russia is better than Michigan!' That was the end of the discussion.

"I, of course, was shocked when this person told me the story, but it gave me an idea. I speak fluent Russian. I have a business degree from one of the top business schools in the US. And if it is true Russia has a 'better' business climate, perhaps I should check it out. So I did. First thing I saw was the Russian business income tax was only 25 percent, and the maximum personal income tax was 22 percent, so I knew I was on the right path to finding a growing economy and more opportunities. I made several trips to Russia and was helped by my parents' relatives who remained. I soon found a position with a Russian oil and gas company that valued my business background and English skills, as many of the exploration engineering companies came from the UK and the US. My positions and pay quickly increased, and within five years I headed up a region in Russia, which was about 45 percent of our total production. I had more money than I knew what to do with and had lavish apartments in Moscow and London, and I spent considerable time in both.

"But then things became what one might call unraveled. The company I worked for was privately owned. A Russian in his forties and his family were the owners, and I was always amazed at how we were able to get these valuable leases on great production areas in Russia. I was not involved in the lease bidding at all. We gave advice to the procurement people on what our chances were in being successful in finding oil and gas in a certain area so they could bid accordingly. And when we signed a lease, then it was handed over to us to find the oil and gas, but again we never did the bidding or negotiation.

"Well, one day the FSB—they're the federal police—raided our Moscow offices and arrested our owner and confiscated all kinds of computers and records. Also, a number of top management people were arrested and taken away. Thankfully, I was in London at the time. Apparently what had happened was the owner and the procurement department had been bribing for quite some time the Russian government officials who were in charge of the lease contract awards. An Asian competitor had upped the ante, which the Russians invited my owner to match. He said no in a not-so-nice way, so they shut him down, charged him with tax evasion, and he is now in prison, and the state took over the business and sold the assets off to the Asians.

"Me, I never went back to Russia. I couldn't get a clear answer as to whether I would be arrested, and it didn't matter, as I had no job there anyway.

"I headed back to New York and put feelers out. I got a job doing research work for a hedge fund managed by Levy and Levy. It involved both taking short positions at times on companies we felt were overvalued but also investing long in opportunities where the product idea and the management were strong. I started focusing on the public utility side, particularly on new technology related to electric power, gas generation and transmission, and water and sewer systems. My timing was good, as most communities were serviced by old technology and publicly managed systems, which were inefficient. Gas, electric, and particularly water and sewer rates were rising each year, well in excess of inflation. So we got wind of some university research on small delivery platforms that actually were quite efficient, as they minimized the transmission costs. We put some businesspeople on the idea. They invested in the technology, sold the idea of privatization to the communities, and started building these micro-utility operations. We even have one here. It's a 125-megawatt nuclear facility, which not only handles Belle Isle, but we also sell the excess to the US and Canadian grids. It's highly efficient. So we provided the capital, and it worked out well for everyone. The Levy partners were very impressed, and when the New York investment crowd got wind of Belle Isle and decided to back it, Levy asked if I would like to establish an operation on Belle Isle and take an equal partnership with them in the company. They liked Belle Isle because it was central in the US, and we could investigate our investment opportunities more readily. When I heard there would be no tax on income and the philosophy of the island would be limited government, I said, or rather shouted, '*Yes!*' So here I am."

Joe broke in, "So has it met your expectations? And do you ever get island fever?"

Yuri smiled. "Two questions. To the first, absolutely. There's an energy and confidence here I have never seen anywhere else. It's liberating to live here. This is truly the land of unlimited opportunity. With the favorable tax system here that doesn't tax income or investment, we have been able to grow the business through reinvestment much more quickly than would have been possible somewhere else. And in the process we have created many high-paying jobs.

"To the second question, hardly. First of all, I am on the road about two days a week. For example, this week I was in Palo Alto, Los Angeles, Fargo, and Wichita on site visits and meeting management. I left early Monday morning and was back here Tuesday night. Because of private aviation, I had only one night in a hotel, as I visited four companies spread all over. Wednesday I went to a Tigers game in Detroit with a friend and then had an early dinner in downtown Detroit. Today I plan to get caught up on my email and paperwork at the office. Tomorrow I'm attending a play at the Performing Arts Center here on the island. Saturday and Sunday are the Gold Cup hydroplane races, and this weekend is just nuts with all kinds of festivities and parties. I'll be watching the races themselves on my boat at the Detroit Yacht Club here on Belle Isle. There's plenty to do here. You know, rather than island fever, whenever I'm away, I miss this place because it is so coooool!"

"Darin and I used to go to the Detroit Yacht Club every summer to watch the hydroplane races from the end of their dock, when we were in high school and college," Joe said. "Darin's dad would get us tickets. It was very exciting to see the boats, but I think the air force jet doing its flight show right above our heads was as exciting as the boat races."

"Well, stick around until Sunday, and you can be my guest on my boat to see it again."

"I wish I could. I'm afraid I can't stay that long."

"I'm sorry. I wish you could too. We have a lot of fun. Here on Belle Isle, we work hard and play a lot, too, and respect both."

Joe reflected on Yuri's enthusiasm and thought that it might be worth another trip back just to watch the races.

They finished their drinks, and Yuri gave them an office tour. Levy and Servenkov had the entire floor. Investment managers had window offices, while the researchers had cubicles in the interior. Joe estimated the size at about fifty offices and workstations. One large room was for the day traders, its walls covered with various video feeds and nonstop scrolling tickers. There were four traders hunched over their computers, while a fifth was napping on a daybed, with his smartphone lying on his chest to waken him if any programmed stops were hit.

Nearby two traders were taking a break, engaged in a lively Ping-Pong match. Yuri commented, "You can't be sitting all day. Need some breaks."

The tour over, Darin and Joe thanked their host and headed for the elevator. They got off at the monorail level; Darin headed back to his office and Joe to the Four Seasons for an afternoon nap, armed with Darin's address in the Residential District for their 7:00 p.m. dinner.

Chapter 19

DARIN'S DINNER

One man with courage is a majority.

—Thomas Jefferson

Joe had trouble deciding what to wear for dinner. Darin had said to make it "dressy casual," whatever that meant. Ultimately he chose to wear his navy-blue blazer over a white button-down shirt, paired with dark-gray chinos and well-polished but comfortable brown leather loafers. He considered adding a pocket square in his blazer pocket but decided against it, as it might look a bit pretentious.

Joe had no problem finding Darin's condo. His smartphone gave walking turn-by-turn instructions, but Joe felt as if he were in a European village with narrow streets and winding alleys. The streets were barely wide enough to handle emergency vehicles but were fine for pedestrians. Some were constructed of large polished gray cobbles, while others were a combination of brick and stone. Attractive wrought-iron streetlamps were spaced along the walkways but didn't have electric bulbs; Joe wondered if they could be real gas lamps. He would have to ask Darin.

A doorman greeted Joe at 33 Rue de Rose. Holding the door open, he asked Joe whom he was visiting. The doorman responded with what Joe surmised was a British or Bermudian accent, "Ah, yes. You must be Mr. Sharif. Mr. Fraser is expecting you. The elevator bank is to your right. Take it to the twenty-fifth floor and exit to your right and go to the end of the hall. Have a wonderful dinner."

Finding the elevator, Joe rode to the twenty-fifth floor, turned right as instructed, and after passing two doors, was greeted by Darin standing in the doorway.

Darin was wearing a tailored charcoal-gray sport coat over a light-blue dress shirt, open at the collar. Paired with the sport coat were dark-indigo jeans, and his shoes were classic black leather brogues. On his lapel was a gold pin, recognizable as the outline of Belle Isle. Joe was relieved that Darin's idea of "dressy casual" matched his own.

"Robert called me and said you were on your way. Welcome!"

Darin's office might have been austere, but his home was not. Not that it was huge; it was just supercool.

The condo was a meld of sleek modernism and minimalistic design. The walls, a blend of soft gray tones and floor-to-ceiling windows, allowed natural light to flood in during the day, casting dynamic shadows across the open-concept living space. The glass reflected the skyline, giving the room an airy, boundless feel.

Italian gray-stone pavers at the entry transitioned into a light oak floor of the great room. The ceiling was also the same light oak. Opposite the entry was a large fireplace with a chimney that rose to the ten-foot ceiling. Both the fireplace trim and chimney matched the stone pavers of the entry.

The furnishings were an exercise in understated luxury: a plush, low-slung sectional couch, upholstered in deep charcoal, centered the living room, with paintings and pictures Darin had acquired in Asia adorning the walls. Every piece seemed meticulously chosen, from the sleek metal coffee table with its glass top to the chrome-finished light fixtures that hung above, casting soft, warm light as the sun retreated to the west.

In the kitchen, leathered quartzite countertops stretched long and uninterrupted, while state-of-the-art appliances in brushed stainless steel gleamed in their precision. The open layout made it feel more like a space for entertaining than simply cooking, with barstools positioned around a floating island, ready for casual gatherings.

Joe noted to himself that Darin's office, with its stark furnishings, and his condo, with its extensive furnishings, were worlds apart. The difference between being a servant and a resident.

Darin poured Joe some Pellegrino, and they settled themselves in chairs on the balcony overlooking the river on the Detroit side. Below them were families packing up from their day at the beach. To the west near the bridge, a large stucco building with a Spanish influence was girded by scaffolding.

Darin followed Joe's gaze. "That's the Detroit Boat Club restoration. The boat club was closed years ago, before the turn of the century, and has really been run down. But it never got demolished, and we decided to let it be. Well, the Detroit Yacht Club, which never closed, had become so successful, and the waiting list for membership was so long, that a group from the wait list got together and bought the old boat club and is now fixing it up. They are keeping the original feel and decor. Just the mechanical, electrical, energy, and technology systems are being upgraded. When they finish, it will be something. They're tearing out all the old docks and putting new ones in, with some docks accommodating one-hundred-foot yachts. I hear the DYC members are a little jealous."

"Do you get boats that big here?"

"Yes, we do. This area is starting to be a jumping-off spot for yachts touring the Great Lakes. They come from Florida mainly. They winter down there and summer up here. They like to explore the North Channel and also do Charlevoix, Harbor Springs, Mackinac Island, even Door County on the Wisconsin side of Lake Michigan. On Lake Huron, they spend weeks in Georgian Bay—it's endless cruising. Some even get up into Lake Superior. A couple of years ago, I went with Yuri on his boat and cruised the North Channel and Georgian Bay. I have *never* seen anything so beautiful. It compares with the Greek islands."

They were interrupted by a call from the doorman. Two more guests were on the elevator. Darin headed to the door and welcomed the new arrivals.

Dr. Priya Desai was a poised and elegant woman of Indian descent, around fifty years of age. She had sharp features and a caramel complexion, and her black hair was streaked with silver, styled in a sleek chignon. She wore a tailored midnight-blue sheath dress with subtle silver embroidery tracing the edges—an homage to traditional Indian craftsmanship. Diamond earrings, a silver bracelet, and low-heeled silver pumps completed her attire. Darin always thought if she weren't a doctor, she could be a model in a women's clothing show.

Jessica Hay was a woman of about forty, with long, curly chestnut-brown hair that cascaded over her shoulders. Her minimal makeup—a neutral rose lipstick and a hint of mascara—enhanced her pale complexion and bright hazel eyes. She wore a tailored charcoal-gray midi dress with a high neckline and three-quarter sleeves, accented with a thin black belt that highlighted her trim silhouette.

The dress was simple yet sophisticated. Pearl stud earrings, a slim Shinola silver watch, black low-heeled pumps, and a structured black leather handbag completed her polished yet unassuming appearance.

Darin introduced the women to Joe.

He quipped with a smile, "Darin Fraser and Jessica Hay. Aren't Fraser and Hay Scottish clans? Have the Scots taken over Belle Isle? Back in time, did they get along?"

Darin was about to answer but was stopped by Jessica's raised hand.

"Actually my great-grandfather was a Fraser. If the two clans fought, it was a very, very long time ago. Today we work together to make Belle Isle the best it can be."

Before they had a chance to settle, the doorman called again to announce a third guest. Hector Cabrera was on his way up.

Darin greeted Hector at the door and introduced him to Joe. Hector was of medium height, with thick dark hair. His skin was quite dark and sun wrinkled. It was hard to gauge his age, perhaps midforties. He wore well-worn dark-denim jeans that showed the faint stains of years spent in the field, though now pressed and cleaned for the occasion. His sturdy work boots had been meticulously polished but still bore the scuffs of a man who worked in the field. A simple olive-green shirt had its sleeves rolled partway up his muscular forearms.

Darin poked Hector in the shoulder. "No 'Hector Time' on dinner invites, my man! Ya done okay this time."

Hector smiled and shook his head. He didn't reply.

Darin looked at Joe, who had a quizzical look.

"Private joke. I'll explain later."

Chapter 20

HEALTH CARE

People are beginning to realize that the apparatus of government is costly. But what they do not know is that the burden falls inevitably on them.

—Frédéric Bastiat

The group retreated back to the balcony, where drinks were served.

"Joe, Priya heads up the Belle Isle Medical Center, and I thought you, being in biotech, might be interested in learning more about her facility. The medical center specializes in the treatment of spinal cord injuries. That's about the limit of my knowledge, although I do know we get patients from all over the world who come here for help. Jessica is the president of Belle Isle and is serving her first term. Hector emigrated from Mexico and has a landscaping business here plus oversees a great charity."

Joe and Priya engaged in technical conversation about the methods employed by the medical center. Darin had heard it many times before but still didn't understand much of what was covered—the use of olfactory ensheathing gia cells, along with the discovery of drugs that are used to counteract growth inhibitory proteins, allowing axon cell regeneration to occur. He and his building design team had, of course, approved the exterior architecture of the medical center, but what happened inside wasn't his forte. But he understood the basics of the health insurance and, when the technical talk wound down, segued to that subject.

"Priya, describe for Joe how we deliver medical services and how it's paid for."

Priya stroked her hair and drained her drink.

"Long version or short?"

Darin replied, "Whatever you want, but let's talk about it over dinner."

They moved to the dinner table, and the server served the first course—a Moroccan chickpea soup.

"Well, first the historical basis," Priya said.

"We all know what happened in the health-care systems of our neighbors. In the US they had excellent care, but it was breaking the budgets and consumed an inordinate amount of the GDP, over 25 percent. Resources weren't allocated with any kind of emphasis on value. There was a disconnect between the patient and the provider. Insurance companies were in the middle, and the patient was blind to the price of the product.

"In Canada the government provided all the care but controlled spending by harsh rationing. If you were young and healthy, it worked fine, but if you got really sick, you had to wait very long times for necessary care, and a lot of people died who could have been saved. Many Canadians skipped across the border to the US if they wanted to get urgent care.

"So we first established the ground rules. First of all, if a person had a congenital condition, then they would receive care. They would pay for it up to a reasonable limit based on their financial ability. So we as a society decided we were committed to spreading the risk of that happening to one of our members. We spread that risk by paying through our taxes for the medical care required over and above what the patient could reasonably pay. And we're talking about residents here. That is one of the benefits of living here in Belle Isle.

"Now we're not necessarily talking about what was called preexisting conditions. Pre to what? If you were born with a defective heart, a new heart would be provided. But if you had poor eating habits and didn't exercise, were obese, and developed type 2 diabetes as a result, then the support was more limited. The patient is expected to do his or her part in creating good health. Second, the patient is fully apprised of the cost of treatment and has primary responsibility for paying for medical services. Now they can purchase insurance, of course, from private companies but are encouraged to carry only catastrophic insurance to cover medical bills they can't afford. And companies don't provide the insurance for their employees on a pretax basis because we have no income taxes here. So people form buying groups to get better rates by bulk purchasing.

"For example, teachers band together to form a group, or accountants do the same. And individuals price before they buy. All our providers issue price lists for things like office visits, surgeries, diagnostic testing, hospital stays, everything. This encourages people to shop and therefore keep the pricing down. Doctors are judged based on metrics such as treatment cure rates and word of mouth. The free market is allowed to function in the medical arena just like every other service. Information using complex statistical analyses has sprung up, some on a freeware basis, which rates the value propositions doctors and hospitals offer. Doctors work on keeping their prices down. And as we have a judicial system here that keeps medical malpractice insurance rates low, the prices tend to be lower. The insurance companies monitor the doctors closely on their malpractice claims paid, which effectively tends to weed out the incompetents."

Joe interrupted, "Yes, Darin and I sat in earlier today on a medical malpractice trial, and he explained how that works. I really like the idea of claims being heard by medical professionals who can render knowledgeable judgments."

The soups were removed and replaced with eggplant rollatini and a sun-dried tomato salad, followed by lamb moussaka.

Priya and Joe continued their shop talk during dinner. Priya described some of the breakthroughs that had occurred in the last five years at the Belle Isle Medical Center on nerve reconstruction. Some patients who came in wheelchairs left walking on their own power.

Chapter 21

THE PRESIDENT

It is incumbent on every generation to pay its own debts as it goes.
—Thomas Jefferson

During the dessert of ginger-brandy cheesecake, the conversation turned from medicine to government. Darin initiated by asking President Jessica Hay to describe for Joe what her day job was like and what duties she was expected to perform.

"Well, the charter is basically to manage and execute on the laws passed by the council, which is our legislative branch. But unlike the president of the United States, I don't set or promote policy. However, I provide advice. If the council is contemplating something that cannot be effectively or efficiently performed, then I weigh in. For example, let's say they were considering passing a law prohibiting chewing gum in public, as is the case in Singapore. I or my staff wouldn't say one way or the other whether we thought this was a good idea, but we would analyze and come up with a probable cost of enforcement, considering both the costs of police and the courts.

"It's a pretty straightforward position. I am a CPA by training, and my primary job is to watch the Midas and keep spending from the inevitable 'creep' that seems to happen to many governments.

We spend some time on compiling metrics of various types to make sure we are always in the top 10 percent of governments in terms of efficiency and thriftiness. The number of government employees per capita is a big one. Also, public expenditures per capita are another, although we have to factor out some of the expenses we have here, such as the monorail, which most other communities don't have. But when it comes to police, fire, courts, tax collections, and the like, we excel in all those areas.

"A third metric is public expenditures as a percentage of GDP. Did you know that the US was spending only 3 percent of GDP in 1929, and it rose in the Great Depression to 10 percent? But in the twenty-first century, it has often exceeded 20 percent. We don't want to repeat that mistake, so we have a goal of less than 10 percent, and we stick to it."

"So how long do you serve, and how did you get elected or appointed?" Joe asked.

Jessica replied, "The term is four years but subject to a recall process, which *can* happen. If a petition comprising 25 percent of the residents is submitted that calls for a recall, then an election is scheduled within thirty days on the issue of recall. If a supermajority of the voters authorize the recall, then the president resigns immediately, and the vice president assumes the office on a temporary basis. A new election is scheduled ninety days out. The two top vote getters then have a second runoff election thirty days later to elect the new president. The recalled president is eligible to run, by the way."

"So your job is to keep the island running, right?"

"It's somewhat more than that," Jessica replied. "Yes, I oversee the public services group, which keeps the streets clean, the garbage picked up, and the monorail running. We actually use private firms for those functions and bid it out every other year. Same thing for the maintenance and janitorial of the publicly owned buildings. We have a procurement function, which handles those things. Police, fire, and taxation fall under my jurisdiction, as do the maintenance and administration of the courts, legislature, and jail. Of course the judges themselves are independent, as is the legislature. So we have three branches of government similar to the US and many states—legislative, executive, and courts. We also have the anticorruption group, which is overseen jointly by the president and the legislature. We refer to it as the ACG."

Chapter 22

LEGISLATORS

It will be of little avail to the people that the laws are made by men of their own choice if the laws be so voluminous that they cannot be read, or so incoherent that they cannot be understood—or undergo such incessant changes that no man, who knows what the law is today, can guess what it will be tomorrow.

—James Madison

"How are the legislators elected, and how long do they serve?"

"We have nine legislators. We call them council members. They have staggered terms of six years and elections every two years. So each election, three are up for reelection. We have term limits, so nobody can serve more than two terms. Members are paid 500 Midas per month. That figure is based on what we estimate the average hourly wage of an islander is times the hours spent on island matters. Being a council member is a part-time job. All of our members have other activities, such as a full-time paid job or caring for their children or whatever. We definitely have resident legislators."

President Hay continued, "The same recall mechanism applies to council members. If 25 percent of the residents sign a recall petition, then a vote is held, and a supermajority of the voters can recall the member. If that happens, we have a special election to fill the position and a second election to decide among the two top vote getters of the first. The new member serves out the remaining term of the recalled member."

Joe had questions. "You mentioned the anticorruption group. I assume they keep government clean, and you mentioned there was joint oversight, but how does that all work?"

"The ACG reports to the three council members who are elected at large, one from each staggered term. The fourth member is the president. So the four of us oversee the process. First, we have policies and procedures to prevent corruption. We think it's much better to prevent it than to fix it after the fact. We use methods that are used in banks and security agencies such as dual signatures, mandatory two-consecutive-week vacations, annual polygraph testing, and a whistleblower call-in number, among others. Everyone in the public service is subject to these measures, including the president and executive branch, the council members, and the judges. We have two full-time people and one part-time person in the ACG."

Darin added, "There are two things that always sink any ship—crime and corruption."

Chapter 23

JUDGES AND COURTS

When a man assumes a public trust, he should consider himself a public property.

—Thomas Jefferson

"How about the judges? Are they appointed or elected, and how long do they serve?"

"The judges are appointed. Electing judges tends to lead to corruption. Their decisions are often slanted in favor of the people or groups that support their campaigns. In studying judicial systems around the world, elected judges are 'redistributionists' They take your money and give it to their supporters. Not blatantly or always but enough to sow distrust in the system.

"When we appoint judges, there are two questions that need answers: Who does the appointing, and how long will the judge's appointment last?

"The judges are appointed by a commission composed of four representatives selected by the Judges Appointment Commission and four representatives selected by the president. Half of the representatives are lawyers and half nonlawyers.

"They serve until the retirement age of seventy. Judges can be recalled by resident petition with a supermajority of the voters."

President Hay continued, "We have three courts. The Ordinary Court is the first level. It tries the criminal cases and hears the civil cases as well. We have two full-time judges and five part-time judges.

"The second level is the Court of Appeals. This has five judges and five substitute judges. Any appeal is heard by the full contingent of five judges. The Court of Appeals will hear appeals from cases of the Ordinary Court and serve as the primary court for any legal actions brought against the decisions or works of the government. So let's say the council passes a law prohibiting chewing gum in public, as is the law in Singapore. A private resident could file an action in the Court of Appeals against this law.

"The third court is the Constitutional Court. This court has five judges and protects the rights of residents accorded by the constitution and decides in matters of conflict between the executive branch and the council.

"Much of the structure we have here is based on the country of Liechtenstein."

BISTR

Chapter 24

HECTOR CABRERA

Why can't everybody leave everybody else the hell alone?
—Jimmy Durante

Darin cut in, "Jessica, speaking of winding it up, I know Joe is absolutely riveted by this legislator and judge stuff, but I want to tell Hector's story, and the evening is not getting any younger."

Jessica smiled. She knew once she got on a subject, she could be overly detailed and long-winded, but it was in her CPA DNA. She relinquished the chair to Darin.

Darin turned to Joe. "Well, the story starts about fifteen years ago. I was on a mission trip to the Baja area of Mexico, to a town called Vicente Guerrero. It's about a day's drive south of Tijuana. A group of us was taking the week off between Christmas and New Year's to build a house for a family in need. The house was very simple—built out of block, it had two sleeping rooms and a living room. No plumbing or electricity. It was wired for electricity, but there was no service to the area. On the so-called plumbing, we dug a separate hole in the back and built an outhouse over it.

"Hector and his wife and two young children were going to live in the house when it was done. Until then they were living nearby with his wife's aunt sleeping on blankets on a dirt floor. So this was quite an upgrade. Concrete floor, actual beds—big step-up.

"Hector had some construction skills. He could swing a hammer and could speak a little English and was very willing to help. We were amazed at how hard he worked. He would be already working when we showed up in the morning, and believe me, we showed up early. And he worked until dark, then insisted we go back to our motel while he cleaned up and put away the tools and building materials.

"We were there a week, and I got talking with Hector and told him about Belle Isle, how it translated in French to 'Beautiful Island' and how it *was* beautiful, surrounded by clean, fresh water. How the streets were clean and paved with beautiful bricks and the buildings stretched to the sky in their gleaming splendor. How the monorail went around the island above the people's heads. I could see I had Hector's attention.

"Then I told Hector about the people. How we had no crime. That everyone had a job or a role on the island. That we respected everyone's right to be the best they could be. That we treated everyone with respect—there were no majorities or minorities, no classes, no divisions among us, that everyone was rich in spirit. That we were truly the land of unlimited opportunity. Hector didn't understand that term in English, so I had to make a stab at it in Spanish. '*Oportunidad sin limite.*' Hector's eyes narrowed at me, and he said, '*Es lo verdad?*' 'Is this true?' I replied that it was."

Darin looked over at Hector and asked, "Hector, what happened next?"

Hector's eyes were moist, and he remained silent. Darin was sorry for embarrassing his friend as Hector composed himself. He hadn't meant to.

Hector finally replied, "I'm sorry. That was a difficult time for me. I was happy having this new house built for me and my family, but after Darin told me about Belle Isle that day, I knew more than anything else in the world, I wanted to live there. In my mind the streets were paved with gold. So I asked Darin if I could move to Belle Isle. Darin told me most new residents had to bring a lot of money with them, but there were exceptions. Exceptions had to make the case why they should be allowed to become a resident. Exceptions also had to have a sponsor who was already a resident. I asked Darin if he would be my sponsor. Darin said he would consider it, but he asked what I, Hector, would contribute to the island. I told him I had skills with plants and flowers and would make Belle Isle, with all its water, even more beautiful than it already was. All I asked was for the opportunity to show him. I must have done a good job with my convincing Darin because here I am!"

Darin put his hand on Hector's arm. "It wasn't quite as simple as that. Hector wrote an essay with my help explaining why he wanted so much to live in a city where the core values of liberty, freedom, beauty, respect for others, unlimited opportunity, personal responsibility, and hard work were promoted. Where government stayed out of the way. I flew Hector up for an interview before the board. He was very nervous, and his English didn't come across so well. The board granted him approval, subject to him having a job lined up here. He moved here about six months later.

"After Hector and his family relocated, he worked for the company that had the trash removal contract with Belle Isle. He did that for over two years. It was a tough job. The trash removal takes place between 3:00 a.m. and 7:00 a.m. because of the vehicle restrictions. So he would get home about 10:00 a.m. after taking the trash to a landfill in Michigan, get some sleep, then study local horticulture. Hector had all kinds of plants and flowers he would grow in his small plot in one of our parks that he leased for a small amount from the city. Hector experimented with different techniques and soils, seeds, fertilizer, and arrangements. Over a couple of years, he had become an expert in not only designing but building gardens of exceptional beauty.

"Hector got noticed by some Islanders who hired him to do their gardens. So Hector moved trash at night and planted and tended gardens in the day. He worked hard and made enough money to even pay full fare for one of his girls' schooling. The other remained on scholarship for a few more years.

"After about three years on Belle Isle, Hector was able to successfully bid on the plantings and flowers for one of our parks—Parc de Leon. We have five parks on the island and bid them out every two years. It was a design/build project, and Hector did a wonderful job. This gave him some extra points when bidding on other parks. He now has Parc de Leon and the Casino park. The Casino park is the one next to the Four Seasons hotel and is our monument park, so that one is a big deal.

"Well, between his two big park contracts and the private homeowners business, Hector has quite an operation going. In fact, he is the largest summertime employer on the island. How many people do you have working for you now?" Darin turned to Hector.

"About 160."

"How many are kids?"

"All but five."

Darin continued, "During the summer they all show up at Parc de Leon at 8:50 a.m. He and his foremen give them the tools and instructions and send them to the parks, businesses, and homes for their workday."

Joe asked, "Why 8:50 a.m. rather than 9:00 a.m.?"

Hector said, "I tell them you start work at 9:00 a.m., but if you're not ten minutes early, you're late. The first-timers look at me like I'm crazy, but they soon learn about 'Hector Time'—if you're not early, you're late. And if they aren't there when we leave for the job, there's no catching up. We send them home."

Darin jumped in, "Since almost all the kids on the island work for Hector at some point and go home to tell their parents about Hector Time, *everyone* started using the term 'Hector Time.' It's become so much a part of our culture that most times, people are a little early for their appointments. Nobody waits. Someday we need to build a big clock tower downtown where the clock is ten minutes fast with a picture of Hector on its face!"

Hector flushed deep red, despite his tan. "I am a lucky man."

Joe asked, "Hector, I hope you don't mind me being nosy, but what do you pay these kids? Do you pay minimum wage?"

"I pay them whatever their work is worth. Some get a little more than others."

Darin added, "Joe, there is no minimum wage here. Minimum wage laws foster unemployment, particularly among young people. We follow Singapore's example on this. The parents of these kids, who are almost always well off, are happy their kids are working, learning Hector Time and other good work habits, and making their own money. Whatever they make is secondary."

Hector smiled. "Yes, and I tell the kids, 'You make it, you take it.' Nothing comes out of their paycheck. No taxes."

Darin turned to his friend. "Hector, tell Joe about the charity you and Herbert started."

Hector brightened. "Well, years ago, I was taking a cab in Detroit from the Transportation Center to downtown, and the cab driver asked where I was from. I told him I was originally from Mexico, so he tried out some Spanish on me. His Spanish was so-so, but he really wanted to improve. We hit it off, and whenever I came over to Detroit, I would call ahead and ask for him by name to be my driver. One thing led to another, and we would have a coffee and a bite after he got off work, if our schedules worked out. Well, I learned he had quite an interesting past— in some ways like mine. He grew up in Oak Park. As a young Black man, he hung out with the wrong people, got involved with a gang, ended up doing drugs and selling them. He shot another gang member and spent five years in prison. When he got out, he was running numbers and driving a cab when I met him. I told him about me coming to Belle Isle and what it meant to me, how I was working two jobs and making something of my life. I guess I gave him some hope. He was a real bright guy with numbers. I told him he should go back to school and learn business. He got into Wayne State and put himself through school. I loaned him some money along the way. He went on to get his graduate degree in accounting and then became a CPA."

Darin interrupted, "Joe, you met him this morning. That was Herbert Watson, who heads up our accounting for the Service Center."

Joe was surprised. "That's quite a story. I guess it shows it's never too late to get your life in order."

Hector continued, "Herbert really wanted to work on Belle Isle. He got a job in our tax department here working on valuations. Did that for five years and then applied for residency. I sponsored him."

Joe asked, "You mean Belle Isle actually granted residency to a convicted felon with a drug history?"

Jessica answered, “It certainly is an exception to give resident status to someone with that kind of past, but it can and does happen. We are always looking through the windshield, not the rearview mirror. Everyone should have hope for a better future. It’s up to them to make it better.”

“That’s the idea that sparked the charity Herbert and I created. Herbert and I formed a group called Seeds of Detroit. We take people who share our beliefs in self-reliance and hard work. They work and live on Belle Isle for about two years, so the island culture becomes a part of them. The Belle Isle core principles of limited government, appreciation of beauty, and respect for all human beings become part of their beliefs. During that time they take classes on leadership and business. After two years they go back to Detroit and use their skills to create a better world on the other side of the river.”

“Has it been successful?”

“Very successful. One of our graduates—we call them Seeders—started a program where he trains ‘horticultural technicians.’ They grow flowers and unusual vegetables on plots of urban farms in the Detroit communities. These horticultural technicians grow their products on pieces of land that they rent from the company for a nominal amount, then over time purchase their property using the profits from the sales of their flowers and vegetables. Along with other people like themselves, they form cooperatives to help buy fertilizers they need and then to sell their products on a collective basis. Another Seeder teaches a class in Belle Isle civics to students at the University of Detroit Mercy. I hear it’s always full.”

Chapter 25

THE VIEW

As a taxpayer, you are required to be fully in compliance with the United States Tax Code, which is currently the size and weight of the Budweiser Clydesdales.

—Dave Barry

Joe looked at his watch. "I know it's not even eleven, but I'm still on Bratislava time somewhat, so I'm not going to last much longer."

Darin stood up. "Joe, before you go, how about a little espresso on the balcony? Ya gotta see the view."

Darin led the way through a patio door to a second balcony off the great room. The floor of the balcony was tiled in gray stone, and the walls were white stucco. Gaslight sconces produced a soft glow. Darin turned the sconces to a low setting, and the group leaned against the rail. As Joe watched the sconces flicker, he asked about the streetlights on Rue de Rose.

"Yes, they are real gaslights," Darin informed him. "Whenever we can, we try to use the real thing. Truth in architecture, truth in government. It's all connected."

Joe reflected. He compared his experience at Disney's EPCOT

Center years ago with what he was seeing on Belle Isle. At EPCOT, he thought it was very clever how they simulated the various countries with tinted concrete made to look like brick or stone. But it was faux. Here it was real.

Joe took in the sweeping view before him. To the right across the river was downtown Windsor, whose dominant landmark was the Windsor Casino. Pairs of headlights in motion defined the streets and the fact the city was still alive at that hour. Straight ahead in the distance, white-and-green lights alternately flashed.

"That's Windsor airport. Quite a view, isn't it? I never get tired of it, especially on a warm summer's night. Although I have to tell you, with the infrared heaters going, the spring and fall evenings are terrific too."

A large rectangular glass table with six chairs was centered on the balcony. As the men and women took their seats, the server appeared with a tray of espresso cups, port glasses, and brandy snifters. A return trip brought a bottle of Sandeman twenty-year-old port, Rémy Martin V cognac, and a humidor filled with fine cigars. Joe took a cup of espresso and passed on the cigar, as did the ladies and Hector. Darin and Jessica took a port, Priya a cognac, and Hector a brandy.

Darin square cut his favorite—a Padron 1926 Anniversaire Series. He lit it with his Vertigo lighter.

Priya and Jessica were immediately surrounded by the smoke, causing the ladies to relocate upwind. Priya reminded Darin about the dangers of smoking. It wasn't the first time she had lectured him.

The group repositioned, Darin reached under the table and pressed a button, and the table came to life. It was actually a TV screen. Displayed was an aerial map image of the surrounding area around Belle Isle. A portion of Lake St. Clair, the Detroit River past the Ambassador Bridge, Detroit, and Windsor were marked in faint outlines. A building on Belle Isle, apparently Darin's condo, was marked in a slightly bolder outline. But dominating the screen were small aircraft symbols moving at measured paces in all different directions. Next to each airplane were various numbers. Joe looked in amazement at the table. Next to an air symbol were the characters "BA22," "275," "42," and "DTW-LHR-11:25." Joe looked to the south in the general direction indicated by the symbol and saw a plane's strobe light as it moved from right to left.

Joe asked Darin, "Is that plane off in the distance the one on the screen here?"

Darin took a penlike object that had been lying on the table and pointed it at the blinking light in the south sky. Immediately on the table screen, the "BA22" plane symbol blossomed into an image twice the size and brightness as the others.

"Yep, that's it. That's British Airways Flight 22 going from Detroit to London Heathrow. Its ground speed is 275 knots, and it's climbing through 4,200 feet and estimated to arrive at Heathrow at 11:25 Greenwich Mean Time. This pointer has a directional signal picked up by a device connected to the screen, so it knows where I'm pointing it and identifies the object on the map."

"Amazing stuff."

"Well, it's fun to play with. Did you ever look up at the night sky, see a plane, and wonder where it was going? I don't need to wonder. I just point at it, and it tells me pretty much everything I want to know. This screen is hooked up to a system called FlightAware, and every airplane that is on a flight plan in the world is on here."

Darin touched a control on the screen, and instantly the entire United States was in view, with hundreds of tiny white dots moving in all directions, resembling a swarm of white bees. He touched another control; the view shifted to Japan and Asia, with even more white bees flying randomly.

"I have another program on here that tracks ships. Same thing. See that light there off in Lake St. Clair?" Joe peered to the east through the glass balcony rail and saw a pair of green-and-red lights.

Darin aimed the pointer, and a boat icon flashed big with the name "Arthur Anderson" and "Duluth-Cleveland."

Joe played with the pointer, aiming it at various planes in the sky and looking at the screen for the plane's information. Next week he would be a spot on the screen. He wondered if Darin would be out here looking for him.

The discussion about Belle Isle government was over, replaced by good espresso, good port, good cognac, good cigars, good friends, and faraway places. Below them the Detroit River seductively beckoned.

Darin mused, "You know, from right here, you can sail to anywhere in the world."

Chapter 26

THE LAST DAY

Why is it that statists believe that if you tax cigarettes you will discourage smoking but if you tax work, risk-taking, and capital formation, you will get a healthier economy?

—Lawrence W. Reed

In the distance Joe was starting to make out the palm trees. Their tops were waving wildly in the wind, like magnets drawing him closer. Then the beach appeared. Its sands seemed endless. He was worried about grounding his sailboat as the waters shallowed. No time to do that after sailing for months from Belle Isle. He heard chimes in the distance. Could that be a warning bell indicating a reef?

The chimes grew louder, and Joe opened his eyes. The sun was already up despite it being 7:00 a.m. He killed the chimes on the clock next to his bed and gazed at the ceiling, buying a few minutes before starting on the new day. It had been an incredible visit so far. He was amazed at what great things the human spirit could achieve, if allowed to be in a state of choice rather than force. Free to succeed, free to fail. But most of all, free. Without failure, there can be no success.

He mused how happy people appeared to be on the streets. He wondered if they were happy in the winter, when the weather was cold and daylight was shorter. Joe thought the architecture and gaslights made the streets look enchanted last night. With heated streets and walks, he could see it might not be so bad in the winter. Darin had done a great job, but of course he was first to admit he had plenty of help. He said he was a lucky guy.

Joe joined Darin on the outdoor patio area of the Four Seasons. They served meals outside starting April 1 and going through the end of October, aided by overhead infrared heaters. If the wind were to blow, there were Plexiglas curtains that could be lowered to protect the patrons. But this morning the temperature was seventy-five, and the wind was calm. It was a great spot to watch the boats.

Darin ordered eggs Benedict, while Joe munched on yogurt and granola. Darin shared the day's plans.

"It's impossible to show you everything. There's just too much, but today we'll hit the School/Worship District, the Sports District, and more of the Entertainment District, which includes the theater. Also, I think you might be interested in the Market, the Transportation Center, and Jefferson."

"You're the tour guide. You lead, I follow!"

Chapter 27

SCHOOL AND WORSHIP DISTRICT

Socialism is a philosophy of failure, the creed of ignorance, and the gospel of envy. Its inherent virtue is the equal sharing of misery.

—Winston Churchill

They exited the monorail at the platform marked School/Worship District. There was a commons area, much like a village green, and on it were about a dozen buildings, all of varied design. Joe first saw a mosque, similar to ones in Turkey, with a gleaming gold dome and minarets. Separated by only a hundred feet or so was a church constructed of stone, topped by a bell tower. Brick walks meandered among the buildings, connecting them with the monorail station. There was a reflecting pool in the middle of the commons with a pathway of gray-stone pavers encircling it. The buildings were sprinkled around the perimeter of the pool. It reminded Joe somewhat of EPCOT Center at Disney World because of the way the buildings were located, but there was none of the amusement park faux-facade feeling to it. These buildings were beautiful, and they were real.

Walking around the pool to the left, they passed the church and came to a synagogue. It was generally traditional, although it had a few modern elements to its architecture. Darin explained how the various members of the synagogue argued about whether it should be traditional or modern. As the Belle Isle Architectural and Planning Board had the final say, Darin was able to bring the decision to a conclusion, backed up by some of his Israeli friends who had worked on the Malaysia project with him.

Past the synagogue was a Roman Catholic church. The architecture was traditional, with some elements that reminded one of the Cathedral of Notre-Dame in Paris. Darin explained that Belle Isle was going to be around for a very long time, so he didn't want any architecture that would become dated.

Other Protestant churches and a Hindu temple completed the circuit around the reflecting pool. All were quite different, but none of them felt out of place with one another. They flowed well together.

Joe and Darin came to a walk made of stone that branched off to the east. About two hundred feet past the last church, they came to a three-story brick-and-stucco building with a stone facade. It had a crock-tile roof, and it reminded Joe of some of the buildings he had seen in Turkey on his travels there. Darin remarked that this was a kindergarten-through-eighth-grade school and that it was privately owned. Over the front door, engraved in stone, was "Belle Isle Junior Academy." Across the street was a similar building but done entirely in stone with a slate roof. Its monument sign was in front and read, "Belle Isle Senior Academy" and served the ninth- through twelfth-grade classes.

Darin explained, "We have two K–12 schools on the island. Both are privately owned and operated. Up ahead is the second pair, which are named the 'Friedman Upper School' and 'Friedman Lower School.' Over to the right is the football and soccer field that the schools share, and next to it is the basketball arena, again shared. They share it under a joint operating agreement. The schools work out their practice and game schedules well before the school year starts to avoid conflicts. The other sports facilities on the other side of the walk include a baseball diamond and an indoor hockey arena.

"All the sports facilities are privately owned by organizations that were set up to be what we call donor-led. In the US, there are non-profits that are structured to attract donors because donations to them are income tax deductions. But here we have no income tax, so we don't have that advantage—if you call it that—but the donors are there just the same."

Joe pressed, "Well, why would they donate without the tax break?"

"Because they want to, and it's a great cause. Most of the donors or their kids have used the facilities. It is a nonprofit with a volunteer board, which oversees the operations. They charge expenses to the school users, but it is very low. And the schools sell tickets to their games, which brings in a little bit of revenue for the schools and pretty much covers what they have to pay for the facilities. We also have a few Red Wings and Lions practices here, which are big draws, and they raise funds from spectator sales. So the schools really pay next to nothing for their use."

"Are there any public schools on Belle Isle?"

"No, only the two private schools."

"How much is the tuition?"

"It varies by grade, and the two schools have slightly different pricing. I'm not totally up on it, but I think the early grades are about 8,000 Midas, and the high schools are about 12,000 Midas."

"And these schools are for-profit?"

"No, they're donor-led nonprofits."

"Why nonprofit? I remember you telling me you encourage for-profits."

"We love for-profits, but the nonprofit, donor-led model works well for schools. It makes fundraising much easier, and our residents recognize the need for a well-educated populace."

"But that tuition is pretty expensive. How many people can afford it?"

"I hear 85 percent of the students are paying full fare. You have to remember, our residents pay no income tax. They are well educated, and they make very good money. The median household income here is over 100,000 Midas, and *they take it all home*. Two kids in high school and one in grade school is really no problem for the typical family. Of the 15 percent who have scholarship assistance, they pay a percentage based on their income and some other factors, but everyone pays something. The schools have very involved parents because all the parents are writing checks. There are no free rides."

"How are the schools rated?"

"Very good. On par with Detroit Country Day, Cranbrook, or U of D Jesuit. Many of our kids go to Ivy League schools or good West Coast universities. Our schools have adopted the ten-month-school-year convention, which gives them a leg up on the old agrarian-based system of nine months. All the Friedman School graduates go on to a higher education, much like Country Day students when we were there. But the Belle Isle schools have a somewhat different approach. If a graduate goes on to technical school rather than college, that's fine. About 15 to 20 percent of the graduates go that route.

"Around the corner there—you can't see it from here—is the Belle Isle School of the Technical Arts. We call it Tech Arts for short. There all kinds of skills are taught. We have skilled construction trades such as carpenters, plumbers, and electricians but also stonecutting, fine masonry, and plastering. It's said we have the finest skilled construction trades in North America coming out of here. It goes well with the need for those lost arts here on Belle Isle with our architectural goals and requirements. And with the revival of the Detroit region and its fine homes, there is a lot of work across the river as well. Tech Arts has some terrific computer and communication technician classes, and of course those jobs are in high demand. They also have horticulture training, and many of those people are employed taking care of the many gardens we have here on the island."

They continued along the stone walk. It curved back around toward the monorail.

"I would give you a tour of the schools, but they're closed for the summer. From mid-June through August, the kids are off, although the sports programs go year-round. Many of our residents have summer places in Northern Michigan or Ontario and go there for the summer."

Their conversation was interrupted by the high-pitched whine of a turbine engine off to the west. Joe looked at Darin, his face framed with a question.

"Joe, that must be one of the unlimited hydroplanes. Say, let's stop at the club and take a look."

Darin and Joe boarded the monorail at the School/Worship station and soon were disembarking at the Detroit Yacht Club.

The Detroit Yacht Club, first formed in 1868, had built its fifth and current clubhouse in 1923. Designed in the Mediterranean style, redbrick and beige-stucco walls were topped with a roof of red crock tiles sprinkled with black accents. Above stood a tall flagpole topped with a large pennant of blue background with a white "DYC." The pennant was extended in a stiff breeze.

Using the bridge, they crossed the lagoon and entered the front door under a massive gargoyle of Poseidon.

Making their way in, the men passed a wall with a collage of the many former commodores of the club. Darin pointed out Gar Wood to Joe.

"Gar Wood is perhaps our best-known commodore. He served in 1921 and laid the cornerstone for the current building. He built his fortune by designing and making the hoist system for dump trucks but is best known for winning a number of Gold Cup boat races in the twenties. Back then the boats could do one hundred miles per hour. That was considered very fast at the time."

The bar faced the river. Over it was a collection of pennants from yacht clubs from around the world. The seats were full, but the bartender recognized Darin and called out, "Mr. Fraser, can I get you anything?"

"Tony, thanks. How about two ginger ales to go? My friend and I are going to watch the boats from the dock. How far along are the races?"

Handing Darin the drinks, Tony replied, "They're doing qualifications today, which will establish the heats for Sunday."

Drinks in hand, Darin and Joe took a position at the end of the longest finger dock.

Joe could see to the west a rooster tail plume in the distance, outlined by the Belle Isle bridge and monorail that connected the island to the Detroit mainland.

The hydroplane turned left and proceeded toward the club. As it closed on them, Joe could see the crimson-and-yellow Red Bull colors. The turbine whine became a roar as the boat passed, doing over two hundred miles per hour, its rooster tail proudly following.

The stiff wind brought the remnants down on the men, lightly soaking them. Joe was thrilled.

They stayed for another lap and, now quite wet, retreated back into the club.

"Joe, now that we're properly cooled off, let's go check out the other side of the river."

Darin and Joe boarded the monorail at the School/Worship station. They switched trains at the Financial District station and boarded the next train for the Transportation Center.

Chapter 28

TRANSPORTATION CENTER

You can't get rid of poverty by giving people money.

—P. J. O'Rourke

The Transportation Center monorail soon crossed the Detroit River and arrived at a station marked "Transportation Center." Now in Detroit, they exited through a pair of automatic double doors to see an overhead sign that read, "Ground Transportation" to the left and "Air Transportation" to the right. They followed the "Ground" sign and entered a lobby that had two rental car desks and behind it an "AutoZipcar" directional sign. Going past the rental car desks and turning to the right, they entered a parking deck filled with cars.

Darin motioned his hand over the deck filled with cars.

"These cars are mostly owned by Belle Isle residents. The deck is on Detroit property but on a ninety-nine-year lease with Belle Isle. If someone has a car here, they pay rent to the Transportation Center owner, which is a private company, but rates are approved by the Belle Isle legislature, according to the return on investment standard I talked about before. It works out to about 150 Midas per month.

"We also have a fleet of AutoZipcars here, for people who don't want to have the costs of ownership and parking or just have access to a second car. It is very popular. And of course there is a line of cabs out front too."

They turned around and headed through a door marked "Air Shuttles." Darin picked one of the autonomous cars from the line and motioned for Joe to join him. Darin punched directions into his smartphone, and the car pulled out of the garage onto the surface street.

"Joe, this car is going to take us to the airport, and we'll see Jefferson on the way."

"Darin, what is Jefferson?"

Jefferson Development

Detroit, Michigan

Legend

- Transit Hub
- Major Transit
- Neighborhood Transit
- Neighborhood Center/ Mixed Use
- Rail/Freight

Master Plan

① Multi-Modal Transportation Center
② Retail District
③ Historic District
④ Mid-Rise District
⑤ Residential "Park" Neighborhood
⑥ Parkway/Greenway
⑦ Gateway
⑧ Aeroplex
⑨ Airport Terminal
⑩ Light Industrial Technology
⑪ Research/Office/Commercial
⑫ Jefferson Avenue Mixed Use
⑬ Open Space/Parks/Residential
⑭ Marina/Parks/Residential
⑮ Port

Ⓐ City Center High-Rise
Ⓑ City Center Mid-Rise
Ⓒ Residential/Park/Mixed Use
Ⓓ Education Worship
Ⓔ Marina

Chapter 29

JEFFERSON

The world needs more men and women who do not have a price at which they can be bought; who do not borrow from integrity to pay for expediency; who have their priorities straight and in proper order; whose handshake is an ironclad contract; who are not afraid of taking risks to advance what is right; and who are as honest in small matters as they are in large ones.

—Lawrence W. Reed

Darin explained, "Jefferson is almost as exciting as Belle Isle. Not long after the Belle Isle idea got traction, our team along with many Detroit forward-thinkers put together a plan for an area of Detroit directly north of Belle Isle across the river, which we called Jefferson Community Investment District, named after its major road along the Detroit River. 'J-CID' was a district created to be used as a public-private investment project where Detroit contributed its tax-repossessed land in exchange for an interest in the upside. Private investors put the fresh capital in.

"Jefferson is approximately fifteen square miles. It had a large amount of vacant or abandoned land, which was ideal for building a world-class logistics center, featuring the movement of goods using air, sea, rail, or roads, all in proximity, to serve the world markets.

Jefferson was large enough to allow the creation of one hundred thousand jobs. Investment capital, estimated to be approximately $100 billion, attracted by Belle Isle.

"But before we could get permission to create this district, we had to create a great 'first impression.' The I-94 highway exit at Mt. Elliot was improved to feature a "gateway" entrance into Jefferson and Belle Isle. Grand Boulevard was redone to feature a green beltway, punctuated with a visitors' center and upscale retail to make that wow factor for new visitors. They demolished the eyesore Packard plant and removed it along with other blight. When investors came through our gateway and drove down Grand Boulevard, they were amazed and immediately favorable to what was being done in Jefferson."

The car was taking them through a succession of industrial parks as Darin continued, "Yes, Jefferson was ideal for a world-class logistics and manufacturing center. Not too many spots in the US have the four-legged transportation stool we have here in Detroit. We have great expressways, rail, shipping, and air. Part of the purchase money for Belle Isle was used to build the seaport and relocate some rail lines. Manufacturers flocked to Jefferson, attracted by the inexpensive land and the transportation infrastructure. Many of them were the businesses owned by the Belle Isle entrepreneurs. It was amazing how quickly the area was transformed.

"And the manufacturing jobs created demand for housing. Many new housing communities were built and, with them, the schools, the retail, the restaurants, and all the services that communities need. I'm not sure on the latest population count of Jefferson, but it's well over 150,000."

The car slowed as it approached a large monument sign, "Detroit Aerotropolis." On the west side, large industrial buildings surrounded an open tarmac, where fork trucks were busy loading shipping pallets of manufactured goods and larger shipping containers onto very large air freighters. Over to the east, Joe spied an array of business jets and turboprops and a shining white terminal topped by a steel-and-glass roof.

Darin pointed to them. "Yes, that's where the 'fly-from' businesses are basing their planes. Andrew's company has one of the smaller ones, but it suits his operation just fine."

A business jet was on takeoff roll heading to the north. They stopped and watched as it lifted off and made a left turn. The sun mirrored off the lowered wing.

"What you're seeing here is the old Coleman Young Municipal Airport, originally called Detroit City. It fell into disrepair like so many other facilities in the area. But we built it up by relocating the runway to the west and lengthening it to 11,000 feet. Now we can take off the largest jets with full loads going transcontinental. There's at least one plane a day going to Japan, Korea, Germany, Russia, and South America. Companies that sell overseas snapped up the air industrial park sites.

"Only two miles from here is the shipping port, with rail lines connecting the two. This gives the businesses in Jefferson the options to move their goods inexpensively by sea freighter or quickly by air. Yuri's company manufactures their micro-utility sewage plants here in Jefferson, ships them by boat to the Far East, but when a critical part needs immediate replacement, they ship it by air within hours."

Darin punched new coordinates in his smartphone, and their car did a U-turn and headed back to Belle Isle.

As they reached the Transportation Center, Darin and Joe passed a money exchange. It had exchange rates for many countries, but in bold letters at the top of the chart was "Dollar-Midas." The rate posted was $3.35 to buy and $3.28 to sell.

Joe stopped and studied the rate board.

"Darin, you say the dollar and Midas were at parity about twenty years ago? Did the dollar really drop that much?"

"Compared to the Midas, it did. All the major world currencies have suffered inflation, but the US dollar has suffered more than most since it was essentially delisted as the world's reserve currency in 2030. The US ran such large deficits, and the Federal Reserve started printing money like there was no tomorrow in an unsuccessful attempt to stimulate employment. But all it did was make investors lose confidence and flee the US, especially the Chinese, which made the problem worse.

"The problem with the Fed was it had two conflicting missions—a stable dollar and full employment. The politics of the matter, COVID-19, and some questionable leadership by the Fed chairman and board of governors sent them down the stimulus path, but it didn't work. All they did by throwing money into the system was to undermine the whole capitalist structure. The deficits were so huge, by the time they figured it out, it was too late. The US had its bonds derated, which caused massive inflation for the US citizens and dollar holders. When interest on the debt exceeded the money spent on defending the country, that was a turning point.

"Here, we took a different approach. Our goal has been and will always be zero inflation. That puts us in a very favored status by investors, and we have no problem raising capital, which provides full employment."

They loaded on the Belle Isle monorail and were back in the Financial Center station after a six-minute ride.

Chapter 30

MARKET

Politics is the art of looking for trouble, finding it everywhere, diagnosing it incorrectly, and applying the wrong remedies.

—Groucho Marx

The world would not be in such a snarl, had Marx been Groucho instead of Karl.

—Irving Berlin

The sun was bright as they stepped off the train. Rather than board the Island monorail, Darin and Joe took the stairs up from the platform and walked north across the island to the open-air market. A stone arch emblazoned with the word "Market" marked the entrance. Inside were row after row of tables, most shielded by awnings. Farmers were hawking fruits, vegetables, and flowers; artisans their jewelry; and a few others were showing off their paintings. Joe saw a couple sizing up his-and-her sweatshirts with an outline of the island on the front and a large "Belle Isle" below. After their purchase, the vendor took a picture of them wearing their matching clothing.

As they passed by several food stalls, the rich smell of lamb wafted over them, and Joe's stomach rumbled. Time had passed so quickly, he didn't realize it was already lunchtime. They stopped at a gyro sandwich stall for Joe, while Darin bought a veggie pita. As they munched their food, Joe perused the nearby fruit stand, laden with a colorful array of fresh produce.

"Where does this stuff come from?"

Darin replied, "Some are grown in Greater Detroit. There are several orchards there. Others are grown farther north. They're brought in every day in the early hours during the time motorized vehicles are allowed, before seven in the morning."

The men found a bench open near the market's perimeter and settled there to eat. Joe guessed the temperature must be close to eighty. Although from where they were sitting there was no water view, people-watching was a good substitute. Tourists were wandering about, with cameras in one hand and kids in the other. They could have been from anywhere in the world. Joe played a mind game where he guessed their country of origin. A Swedish couple no doubt—both blonde. Another couple—he with a ruddy complexion and she with red hair. Must be a Brit married to an Irish lassie. A man with a dark complexion and a prominent nose, maybe Croatian? The game was basically idle curiosity, and Joe never found out the actual origin. But it seemed there were many tourists, and Joe heard many languages being spoken.

"Darin, you get a lot of tourists here? I mean, other than people from the Detroit area or Windsor?"

"Many. We keep track. Belle Isle is a big tourist draw, but it's not their only destination. They spend time in Detroit and Windsor too. People see this both as an interesting social experiment and a fun place. What do you think?"

Joe chose his words carefully. "I think it is beyond interesting.

What I see is the human spirit liberated, and the result is amazing. I've been watching the people here carefully. It's sort of a combination of the energy of New York City with the friendliness of the Midwest. I've done quite a bit of travel all over the world but have never seen anything quite like this. I really think you have done something exceptional here."

"I've had help, believe me. Some of the best minds in the world have participated and often asked for little in return. I think what helped us is the original groundwork and vision of a society where government gets out of the way. We just need to protect the field from intruders and let the farmers grow their crops, so to speak."

The sun continued its slow journey toward the west as it warmed the market. Darin suggested they consider going to a play at the Performing Arts Center that evening, but Joe preferred to just have a leisurely dinner and take in the sights, sounds, and smells of the island. It was going to be just too nice to be inside. They agreed to meet in the hotel bar at 7:00 p.m. and then go to dinner.

Chapter 31

CRONY CAPITALISM

Only a crisis—actual or perceived—produces real change. When that crisis occurs, the actions that are taken depend on the ideas that are lying around. That, I believe, is our basic function: to develop alternatives to existing policies, to keep them alive and available until the politically impossible becomes politically inevitable.

—Milton Friedman

Darin was already at the bar when Joe arrived. He looked lost in thought with a hint of a frown, staring at nothing in particular.

"Hey, Darin, what's happening? You look too serious, man. Are you working on some new project?"

"No, I was just thinking about how much time has passed since we last saw each other. It's scary that it happened so quickly. I hope we do better keeping in touch going forward."

"I'm with you on that," Joe said. "Sometimes I think we get so wrapped up in our careers or the day-to-day stuff that we lose focus. Days turn into weeks, weeks into years, years into decades, decades into a lifetime. But you've made the most of it. It's just incredible to me what you've done here. You must be proud."

Darin continued to gaze at nothing. "Yes, I am proud but worried too. Proud that I could be a part of a movement that turned the tide from negativism and paternalism to optimism and individual freedom. But worried that we might slip backward toward elitist so-called experts who know better than the rest of us and letting those people make the rules. And you can bet that once the experts allow the camel's nose into the tent, the stampede of their capitalist cronies on their coattails soon follows."

"But I thought you were pro-capitalism. What are you saying?" Joe asked.

"I am pro-capitalism, as it's based on choice. But I am against those who, in the name of capitalism, use government to give themselves a monopoly or competitive advantage."

"What do you mean? Give me an example."

"Let me think." Darin paused for a bit, then said, "Sure, I'll give you an example. I'm an architect, right? So I get involved in building specifications and codes. Companies that make fire suppression sprinkler heads, piping, and valving have long been lobbying for mandatory inclusion of sprinkler systems in buildings. They do it by funding some study that purports to show that a sprinkled building saves lives. Now I personally don't think so. Smoke detectors, especially the latest generation, which detect a fire before there's even any flame, *do* save lives. Get 'em out of the building! By the time the sprinklers go off, it's pretty late in the game. I agree that often property damage is reduced by sprinklers, although in some cases I've seen some terrible damage from sprinklers going off accidentally. But my point is, the people who are affected—the person paying for the building and the person living in the building—are not consulted on what *they* prefer. The experts know better. No way! The experts are just working for people who are lining their own pockets. That's what I mean by crony capitalism. Of course there are a million other examples. It's not quite hard corruption. Let's call it soft corruption, at least a conflict of interest. I once looked up the dictionary definition of 'corruption.' It was 'perversion of integrity.' That's pretty broad."

Darin's brow was furrowed, and his passion was center stage. Joe had not seen this in Darin before.

"Darin, I know what you mean. I had a recent experience in line with what you're talking about. My firm was working on an enzyme that had success in treating pancreatic cancer in mice. We were ready to put together a human trial, and the equivalent of the Slovakia FDA denied us permission to go ahead. We learned through the grapevine that a competitor, much larger than us, was about to do their own trial on the same disease. They had good connections with the government. We did not."

Darin looked over at Joe. "You know, I see this as a war of sorts. People who sell their souls for a buck. They know what's right and wrong but choose to look the other way. We must ever resist the tendency. I know it's as old as time, but the truly great societies have become great by rising above it. But let's go eat. We can talk over dinner."

Doakes & Sons

Chapter 32

JOBS

My reading of history convinces me most bad government results from too much government.

—Thomas Jefferson

Darin and Joe hopped on the monorail and headed east, getting off at one of the residential stops. Darin suggested they dine at a small bistro overlooking Blue Heron Lagoon called Ten Tables. It was a favorite of the locals, as they could walk a block or two in the morning for coffee and croissants without having to get on the monorail. In the evening it specialized in exotic Middle Eastern dishes, making it a frequent dinner spot for Darin.

As they walked along the cobblestone street toward Ten Tables, Darin and Joe stopped to look at a building under construction. Four stories in height, the front was largely stone with brick-and-stucco accents. The sides were stucco with some block patterns. Joe noticed gargoyles on the front near the roofline. It reminded him of some buildings he had seen in Prague.

Two men were in conversation in the front yard. They noticed Darin and Joe and came over to introduce themselves. One appeared to be midfifties and the other around thirty.

The older one opened with “So how do you like it?”

Joe replied, “It’s beautiful. It reminds me of Prague. Of the cities of the world I’ve visited, Prague is, in my mind, the most beautiful, but I have to say Belle Isle is giving it a run for its money. I’m visiting here, and it is amazing.”

“Thanks, but I can’t take credit for the way it looks. I’m just the builder, not the architect. But we do take pride in how it comes out, and we do our best to make sure our workmanship exceeds what the owner and the architect expect. Say, where’re you from?”

“I live in Slovakia, but I was born and raised in the Detroit area. I’m visiting my friend here who lives on Belle Isle. He’s giving me the full tour. I’m Joe Sharif, and this is Darin Fraser.”

“Joe, good to meet you. I’m Calvin Doakes, and this is my son Claudio. And, Mr. Fraser, of course I know who you are. It’s an honor to meet you.”

The men shook hands. Darin said with a warm smile, “Darin works just fine.”

Joe could see the family resemblance. Both were good-looking men of African descent and had the same square jaws, just Calvin had a sprinkle of gray hair.

Joe asked, “So, Calvin, there sure seems to be a lot of construction around here. Have you been a part of it?”

“Yes, sir, I have. I got started here about twenty years ago, when Belle Isle got really going in a big way. I’m from Detroit, and before Belle Isle came along, I didn’t think there was any hope for me. I was on Section 8 and food stamps and any other government program I could find, but I just knew my life was going by. What was I going to be remembered for when I was gone? It really bothered me. Then Belle Isle was sold, and they started doing all sorts of construction work. There was a trade school in Detroit, which was supported by the purchase. I took classes there—they were cheap—and I learned carpentry, drywall, and plastering. Then I got a job on Belle Isle doing that kind of work and started making some real good money. I got off the government programs, still saved money, and then bid on some of the work under my own name. I started my company, 'Doakes and Company.' Man, I can't tell you how proud I was when I got my business cards and letterhead back from the printer, seeing my name on it. I was a somebody finally. What a feeling. I not only had money, but I had *dignity*.

"I got more and more work, then became a general contractor, not just a carpenter and finisher, and started doing the whole building. Now I think I've built almost fifteen hundred homes or condos on Belle Isle. And 'Doakes and Company' is now 'Doakes and Sons.'" Calvin gave Claudio a one-armed hug and grinned. Claudio looked embarrassed.

Darin interjected, "And Sons. So, Claudio, do you have a brother in the business?"

"Not yet. I have a younger brother in school still getting his business degree, but I guess he knows there's a spot for him if he wants it."

"That's a great story, guys. So Belle Isle has really helped you. Started a business, turned into a family business," Joe observed.

Calvin answered, "It's not just the Doakes family. There were so many construction jobs created, it was just unbelievable. At the peak, there were twenty thousand workers on Belle Isle doing construction. We had regularly scheduled buses from all over Detroit that were running directly onto the island to move Detroiters to the construction. These buses were set up only for the workers. There were so many of them. Now we don't take buses onto the island, as

Belle Isle doesn't allow them as they did in the construction boom period. We take the ferry. But during the heyday, it was crazy. A lot of my friends made a lot of money doing construction, and many started their own businesses.

"Yes, Belle Isle is largely getting built out. But the second boom is in Detroit. Now most of my business is in Jefferson across the bridge. I built twenty-two homes there just last month."

Darin glanced at his watch and said, "Calvin and Claudio, thanks for sharing your story with us, but Joe and I have a dinner reservation we have to get to. You guys take care."

They shook hands, and Joe and Darin walked another block east to the restaurant.

Chapter 33

THE LAST SUPPER

First they ignore you, then they laugh at you,
then they fight you, then you win.
—Mahatma Gandhi

Ten Tables was located in the basement of a four-story brick building with apartments above. One could easily miss the entrance, as it was on the side of the building and not visible from the sidewalk. The low ceilings gave it a snug, cozy feel, and the dim sconce lighting cast flickering shadows. The decor was eclectic; perhaps one could say the decorating was "Early Garage Sale." Mismatched wooden tables and chairs added to the charm. The walls were a patchwork of exposed brick, quirky artwork, and antique mirrors. A small bar sat at one end of the room, its surface cluttered with bottles of wine. The menu was handwritten on a chalkboard. The lamb tagine with apricots and almonds looked good to Darin, and the beef *kofta* with yogurt sauce appealed to Joe.

The hostess directed Joe and Darin to a table off in a corner. She knew it was Darin's favorite.

The soup of the day was a *harira* soup, a Moroccan soup made with lentils, chickpeas, and tomatoes and infused with cinnamon, cumin, and ginger. They resumed their discussion over the soup.

"So you were talking about capitalism and cronyism," Joe reminded Darin.

"Yes. My point is that a society that doesn't respect individual freedom, that holds an elitist view that the common man can't make good decisions in the face of expert opinions, that the experts must make laws to protect the common man from his poor decisions, becomes a society that is easily manipulated by the clever among us to their own advantage. The few manipulators become very rich, and we who are manipulated become a little poorer. But with each occurrence, the cumulative effect is we become quite poor or at least never become as wealthy as we otherwise could.

"The manipulators are very canny. You've heard a picture is worth a thousand words. Well, an anecdote is worth a thousand statistics. How many bad laws have been passed because of one person's tragedy? Just look at the laws in the US that have been passed with someone's name attached to it. The politicians say look at the polls—the majority wanted it. But majority rule, by its very nature, stops innovation and experimentation. Majority rule is status quo. And the longer the tenure of the status quo, the tougher it is to make a substantial change. F. A. Hayek, the Austrian economist whom we have named one of our streets after, said it well: 'It is always from a minority acting in ways different from what the majority would prescribe that the majority in the end learns to do better.'"

Joe said, "It seems like what you've created here on Belle Isle would work in a lot of other places as well."

Darin replied, "I think some of the aspects of this society *have* been adopted. There is no doubt Detroit and its neighboring cities have greatly benefited by our example. Many say that is why Detroit has roared back. Whether others will pick up and follow our lead, it's hard to say. I guess time will tell. But we are basing what we do on a few core principles, which, I believe, are universal truths that many cultures can use," Darin replied.

"Like what?"

Darin considered his answer. "Number one—keep it simple. Not because people are stupid. They're not. It's just because when you have a lot of complexity, such as a two-thousand-page piece of legislation, society needs experts to tell the common man what it means, and the experts, once in the game, magically transform into elitists. And the simple principles of accountability and responsibility are thrown to the winds.

"Number two—if you have a dog in the hunt, go to the sidelines."

"What the heck does that mean?" Joe asked.

"It means if you're in government and your vote has some positive outcome for you personally, then recuse yourself. For example, you shouldn't be allowed to vote on your salary or whether your job should be continued. You shouldn't be allowed to vote to help some corporation or industry that contributes money to your campaign. You shouldn't be allowed to vote on public union issues when the unions are backing you financially. These are or were issues in the US. There are, of course, many more examples. We don't have those issues here."

Darin continued, "Number three—allow charity to flourish. *Americans are the most generous people in the world.* Belle Islanders are even more so. But the government, through its social programs, crowds out charity. People don't see the need if the function is being performed by the government. They also don't have the extra money to give to charity if it's been already taken by taxes. That's where we have really excelled here on the island. People who are taxed against their will and the money given to others without the giver's input feel a lot of resentment about the process and, in many cases, the recipients. But those who are given the opportunity to freely give feel good about themselves and feel positive toward those who are the beneficiaries. It's a win-win. One of my favorite sayings regarding taxes and charity is 'At least they could ask!'

"Number four—everyone needs to have skin in the game. All residents, unless they are truly unable through no fault of their own, such as the mentally impaired or disabled, need to pay something toward what they receive. People do not value that which is given to them. They do value and take care of things they either own or items they paid for. Take education as an example. Who studies harder on the average—the kid who puts himself through school with his own money earned by summer jobs or the kid whose parents have picked up the whole bill?"

Darin continued, "Number five—don't spend more than you take in. Seems pretty simple, doesn't it? But look at all the countries in history that didn't follow that rule until it was too late. Even the US, once the richest country in the world, didn't balance spending with taxation where it had the resources to easily do so. Now the dollar isn't worth squat, and Americans are generally poor, at least in our view."

Joe asked, "Is that it? Is there more?"

Darin replied, "Yeah, there is one more thing that America sometimes seems to forget, and it's the set of principles on which both America and Belle Isle were built.

"Freedom and opportunity excite people and seem to bring out the best in our species, and capital follows these and the competitive advantage that flows from them. This is what creates the jobs and the lives our people really want.

"Freedom and opportunity—that's it."

Joe had never experienced before the feelings that were now swirling in his head. Listening to Darin and seeing for himself what had been built gave him an optimism that displaced some of the cynicism that had developed over the years. He compared Belle Isle's friendly unity with the polarization in Slovakia and the United States. Could it spread?

As Joe mused over this, the main courses were served, and they changed the subject to old high school and college memories. Darin always felt engaging in political discussions during dinner was bad for his digestive health.

They split a baklava cheesecake and then decided to walk outside after they had finished. The streetlights were a combination of softly glowing electric lamps and gaslights. The beauty of the setting gave Joe an inner peace as he and Darin strolled the two blocks to the monorail station.

Joe felt as though the buildings, with their diversity of unique designs, stood as a monument to all the best human qualities—passion for beauty, freedom to work hard and keep the fruits of your labor, and respect for others to do the same. It had been quite an experience for him, and he wasn't anxious to return to Bratislava, where life wasn't bad, but it certainly lacked the energy and optimism that he saw here. In Slovakia, people still labored under the post-Soviet mindset. It was better than it used to be, but the government and regulators still reigned supreme. Belle Isle was different.

Perhaps it really was the Shining City in the River.

The men boarded the monorail and headed back to the Four Seasons. They disembarked and rode the escalator down to the lobby. Darin and Joe embraced.

"My place is close by, so I'm going to say my goodbyes here," Darin said.

"And have a safe drive up to Petoskey tomorrow. You'll be seeing family, right? And when you head back to Bratislava next week, I hope you take back with you some of the ideas you picked up here in Belle Isle. You know we don't have any copyrights or pride of authorship. Feel free to steal anything you wish!"

Joe took a deep breath and slowly exhaled.

"Darin, I don't want to take advantage of an old friendship in any way, but I have a question."

Darin put his hand on Joe's shoulder. With a welcoming smile, he looked directly into Joe's eyes.

"Sure, anything."

"I've been thinking. Would it be possible to move our Boston operation to Belle Isle? Is there room? Being in the center of the country with better access to our markets, the ease of transportation, the taxation system, but perhaps most of all, the culture. The freedom to make a great life. And this is where I want to live. I want to be a part of it."

A smile spread across Darin's face. "Joe, Belle Isle would be better for it. We would be happy to receive your application. On Belle Isle, your business will grow more than you can imagine or dream.

"Anything is possible here."

EPILOGUE AND ACKNOWLEDGMENTS

Throughout history, time and time again, we have seen how one person can influence a community or region to a much greater degree than logic would dictate. In the case of Detroit, Cadillac was the first to settle the city in 1701, later followed by Woodward a century later with his system of street design, and then Henry Ford, with his innovative manufacturing systems.

The Freedom City of Belle Isle is not a person in the sense of Cadillac, Woodward, or Ford. But it can provide the "change agency" that is so desperately needed for Detroit at this point in its history. I know the reader is probably thinking, "Good luck getting this done." But don't underestimate the power of an idea. The Declaration of Independence and its sentiment, "We hold these truths to be self-evident, that all men are created equal, that they are endowed by their Creator with certain unalienable rights, that among these are Life, Liberty and the pursuit of Happiness," inspired a ragtag army of five thousand rebels to defeat the most powerful nation of its time. As mentioned in the introduction, Mahatma Gandhi did the same thing without firing a shot. He brought down colonialism with the power of the idea that we all have a divine right to freedom, sovereignty, and self-determination.

Detroit badly needs something to lead it out of its depression. The $1 billion would solve a lot of budget problems and could be used fruitfully for relocation expenses, as neighborhoods will need to be consolidated. The concept of Belle Isle will attract people from all over the United States, Canada, Europe, Asia, and South America who will want to live in the community, not only for its freedom and good governance but also because it is centrally located in the largest economy in the world. The influx of these people will bring Detroit back, as they are not going to spend all their money or time on a one-thousand-acre island. Their economic influence will extend far beyond Belle Isle.

If done right, the Four Seasons hotel will become an icon to the world, just as the Opera House has to Sydney, Australia. Photos of Detroit will always include a piece of Belle Isle showing the Four Seasons. You can count on it!

The reader may ask, "How much is fact, and how much is fantasy?" For those readers not familiar with Detroit, Belle Isle is a real place and is accurately described in terms of size and location. The main characters, Joe and Darin, are based on real people, as is Darin's brother, Andrew. Hector Cabrera is based on a real person from the Baja Peninsula village of Vicente Guerrero. The Friends of Liberty are a real group and have already made significant contributions to improving Michigan society. The Mackinac Center is a real think tank, and the article "For Whom the Private 'Belle' Tolls" was a real one. Although Yuri Servenkov's character is fictional, his story about the Phoenix aircraft supplier and Michigan's reputation is entirely true.

I want to thank some of the people who have contributed reviews or advice on this novella. My liberal Ann Arbor friend Doug Turner gave me sound advice, after reviewing an early draft, to make sure Belle Isle did not become a rich man's gated island. That is certainly not my intent, and I hope the reader can see that.

David Littmann, former chief economist of Comerica Bank and currently an adjunct scholar with the Mackinac Center for Public Policy, spent considerable time educating me on the Scottish free-banking system. I didn't use that concept entirely but did adopt the principle of private bank insurance. David also suggested the Belle Isle currency be 100 percent backed by a basket of commodities rather than simply one, such as gold.

Manny Lopez, formerly with the *Detroit News*, provided substantive advice in the philosophies and approaches of the book.

Harold "Hal" Sperlich, former president of Chrysler Corporation, was the father of the Mustang, K-car, and minivan and a great visionary. In 2009 Hal was inducted into the Automobile Hall of Fame as "the greatest automobile designer of the twentieth century." Hal reviewed the manuscript and inspired me to think positively about the possibility of actually making this happen. Hal also commented after reading an early manuscript that Belle Isle is all about "unlimited opportunity." So I have incorporated that label many times in the final copy. I also want to thank Hal for sharing his enthusiasm for the book by penning the commentary section.

The late author P. J. O'Rourke contacted me after the first edition of *Belle Isle* was published. He visited with me in Detroit, toured Belle

Isle, offered his encouragement, and wrote a piece about the idea that was published in the *Wall Street Journal*. For that I am most grateful.

Randy Barnett, law professor at Georgetown University, has offered advice on the Belle Isle concept. Randy advised that my original concept of Belle Isle becoming a commonwealth would face too many constitutional hurdles. Thus the pivot to a Freedom City that can be done legislatively.

I hope the reader shares Hal's, P. J.'s, and my optimism. Big problems need big solutions. Nibbling on the fringes won't make it happen.

These mighty gifts—freedom and self-determination—can be ours once again. All we need are three signatures to enable the miracle—the mayor, the governor, and the president.

Simple, really. That's all it takes. The rest will unfold from the power unleashed.

Rodney Lockwood
January 2025

How to Obtain More Information

At the website below, you can find out more about the Belle Isle concept and how to become involved, including a short video.

www.belleisle-freedomcity.com

The author may be contacted at rlockwood@belleisle-freedomcity.com.